BRENT LIBRARIES

Please return/renew this item
by the last date shown.
Books may also be renewed by
phone or online.
Tel: 0333 370 4700
On-line www.brent.gov.uk/libraryservice

D0263156

The Runaways

Holly Webb

SCHOLASTIC

Published in the UK by Scholastic Children's Books, 20XX
Euston House, 24 Eversholt Street, London, NW1 1DB, UK
A division of Scholastic Limited.

London – New York – Toronto – Sydney – Auckland
Mexico City – New Delhi – Hong Kong

SCHOLASTIC and associated logos are trademarks and/or
registered trademarks of Scholastic Inc.

Text © Holly Webb, 2019
Illustration © Lucy Davey, 2019

The right of Holly Webb to be identified as the author of this work has been
asserted by her under the Copyright, Designs and Patents Act 1988.

ISBN 978 1407 19190 4

A CIP catalogue record for this book is available from the British Library.

All rights reserved.
This book is sold subject to the condition that it shall not,
by way of trade or otherwise, be lent, hired out or otherwise circulated in
any form of binding or cover other than that in which it is published. No
part of this publication may be reproduced, stored in a retrieval system,
or transmitted in any form or by any means (electronic, mechanical,
photocopying, recording or otherwise) without prior
written permission of Scholastic Limited.

Printed by CPI Group (UK) Ltd, Croydon, CR0 4YY
Papers used by Scholastic Children's Books are made
from wood grown in sustainable forests.

1 3 5 7 9 10 8 6 4 2

This is a work of fiction. Names, characters, places, incidents
and dialogues are products of the author's imagination or are used
fictitiously. Any resemblance to actual people, living or dead,
events or locales is entirely coincidental.

www.scholastic.co.uk

For Ash, Robin and Will

BRENT LIBRARIES	
EAL	
91120000418333	
Askews & Holts	04-Oct-2019
JF	£6.99

Chapter One

Molly pushed open the door of the shop, and flinched a little at the bright jingle of the bell. No one went in or out without her mother knowing. She breathed in the familiar sharp smell of new fabric, mothballs and the greasy undertone of knitting wool, and slid hopefully towards the counter, and the door that led to the storeroom and the tiny flat beyond.

"And where exactly have you been, miss?" Her mother leaned over the counter and gestured at her with the knitting she held.

Molly widened her eyes innocently. "School. You know I have, Mum. We had to go and practise for the evacuation. Same as every day this week."

"Yes, and I know that half the other children in the street were back hours ago," her mother snapped. "You've been off messing around with those other girls. Look at the state of your dress!"

Molly hurriedly brushed at the streaks of dust that ran down the skirt of her pale blue cotton dress. She was far better dressed than most of her friends, since her mother had all sorts of odds and ends of fabric she could use up to make her clothes, but sometimes she longed for one dark, sensible dress that didn't look dirty as soon as she'd walked down the street in it. "Sorry, Mum. I must have brushed up against a wall. . ."

"Where were you?"

"Just in the park, chatting. Talking about what's going to happen." Molly looked at her pleadingly. It had seemed like the perfect chance for a little bit of freedom – a little time away from the shop and

Mum always having to know exactly where she was – but she had forgotten that Mum would see the others coming back.

Molly twisted her fingers together behind her back, trying not to let the corners of her mouth lift. Sally and Jean had been crying in the park. They didn't want to be evacuated – or they did, but they wanted their whole families to go; they hated the thought of leaving their mums, both of them. Molly had tried to say that at least they'd all be together. She thought they would, anyway. Miss hadn't seemed absolutely sure where they were going, but she'd said everyone in the school would go to the same place. That was how it was supposed to work. Molly had sniffed a little and tried to look sad when Sally and Jean were so upset, but really she was ... excited. She'd never been out of London. She'd hardly ever been further away than their school. And as soon as school was over, she always had to go straight home, with no dithering about. It had always been the same – but now it was going to be so, so different. She loved her mum – of course she did – but that didn't mean she had to be two steps away from her every waking hour. Anyway, in a few days' time, who knew where she would be?

No one really knew what was happening, not even the teachers. Were they going to be evacuated or not? Miss kept scurrying about with lists and letters and scraps of news, but no one was sure. All they'd done that morning was sit on the floor of the school hall and sing while the staff huddled in corners and eyed bits of paper. It had been the same all week, but today there had been whispers running round.

"Miss reminded us about what we had to bring again," Molly ventured now. "She said you had the list. Indoor shoes. And a flannel, and ... I can't remember it all. There was a list..." She could remember, really – she could have recited the list like a poem. But her mum's face was so flat and closed, it seemed better to pretend.

"It's here."

Stella spoke from the door to the back room. "In that pile of papers under the tea caddy. I can get it."

Molly darted a grateful glance at her sister. Miss had said they needed as many of the things on the list as their parents could spare. In a suitcase. Or a pillow slip would do, Miss had added hurriedly as the children stared back at her. Molly knew that there was a little suitcase on the top of the cupboard on the landing upstairs, if only Mum would listen to her. Molly had everything on the list, which half the children in her class didn't. But Mum hadn't got any of it ready. Sally's mum had pawned her Sunday dress so that she could buy Sally a nightie and her brother Pete pyjamas, because the list said nightclothes and Sally and Pete slept in their vests. She had packed them an old kitbag of their father's every morning that week, and they'd lugged it to school. No one knew when the order to evacuate would be given, but they were supposed to be ready.

Molly had read the list when they were first sent it. Mum had muttered and hissed and snorted about it as she bagged up reels of cotton and counted change in the shop, and that night Molly had lain in bed, ticking off everything in her head, and imagined packing it in a neat little case. But the case was still on the cupboard shelf, and her shoes weren't shined, and her cardigan had a hole in the elbow. She had taken a brown paper parcel with spare socks and handkerchiefs in it to school every morning that week, along with her coat and her gas mask, but she didn't feel ready at all. It was almost as if she wasn't going anywhere.

Perhaps Mum was going to miss her so much that she didn't want to get the things ready?

Molly looked up at her mum uneasily. What if she ended up on a train with just the scruffy brown paper parcel? It had come undone again a few times, and she'd nearly lost her clean socks in the park.

"I could reach that little case down," Stella suggested. "The one from the cupboard upstairs. She could take that, couldn't she?"

There was a scrabbling noise and a pattering of paws, and Mum whipped round. "Don't let that dog in here!"

Stella fielded Bertie expertly, catching at his collar, and Molly knelt down to fuss over him. She scratched him under the chin and threaded his soft ears through her fingers until he leaned floppily against her leg, eyes closed in delight.

"Did you take him out?" she asked Stella, and her sister shook her head, just a tiny twist and a sideways look to their mum. So Bertie had been stuck in the kitchen all day. He must be desperate for a walk. Stella had probably let him out to pee in the yard, but it wasn't the same.

"You're not disappearing off out again," Mum said to Molly as she eyed the dog disgustedly. "Put him in the yard, and come back here."

"He needs a walk," Molly tried, but her voice faded away, and Stella flapped a hand to tell her to hurry on out.

Molly hung up her gas mask on the hook by the back door, and shooed Bertie gently into the paved yard. She glanced hopefully around the kitchen, but there wasn't anything she could snatch to eat. She hadn't had anything to eat since breakfast – and that was a bit of bread and marge before she'd gone out to school – but now wasn't the time to mention being hungry.

The bell rang again as she slipped back into the shop, and a woman she vaguely recognized from down the road came in, looking flustered. "Do you have any black material, Mrs Mason?"

Molly's mother sucked in a breath.

"I need to make blackout curtains," the woman went on. "Or blinds, I suppose." She looked rather helplessly around the shop. "I kept meaning to get the fabric when they had the practices, but, well... My neighbour heard on the wireless that the blackout's in force from tomorrow, so I can't hold off any longer."

The woman's stockings were a mass of darns, Molly noticed, and there was a tiny split just starting to show in the side of her shoe. Molly wondered what she would have to go without, to afford the material to cover her windows.

"We only have the dearer stuff left," Molly's mother said, "but of course it's thicker, so it's a good investment in the long run. A very nice black sateen, three shillings a yard."

"Oh. . ."

"Burford's down the road has black paint," Stella put in, ignoring their mother's dark look. "You can just paint your windows. If, um, it's not a good time to buy the fabric."

"Paint?" the woman murmured, blinking worriedly at Molly's mother, who was still glaring. "But . . . then it would be dark all the time. We'd need lights on in the day as well."

"Yes," Stella admitted. "But it's what a lot of people are doing – it'll save having to put blinds up."

"False economy, dear." Molly's mother shook her head. "You'll be putting money in the electric, hand over fist."

"I'll take two yards," said the woman as she pulled a purse out of her battered handbag and counted out the six shillings in reluctant pennies and tuppences.

The girls' mother turned on Stella as soon as the shop door was shut. "What were you doing, telling her to buy paint? You haven't the sense you were born with!"

"It's the war effort," Stella murmured, shrugging helplessly. "Besides, she wasn't going to buy any more than that, Mum. You could see she didn't have the money."

"If she doesn't paint her other windows, she'll be showing a light and we'll all be for it," Molly pointed out. "She only lives a few doors down. Bill Harper says the Germans have got bombs that can blow up half a street."

"I haven't forgotten you were off gallivanting

about for hours," her mother snapped. "You two had better go and sit in the storeroom and wind all this wool."

Molly didn't complain, though she did glance back towards the kitchen and the little paved yard, worrying about Bertie, still shut outside. Most people let their dogs out on the street by themselves, but Molly was too worried about Bertie getting knocked down, or kicked by a horse. He didn't understand roads at all. Stella ought to make more effort to stand up to Mum and take him for a walk in the middle of the day – it was because of Stella that they had him, after all. A surprising number of young men came to Mason's, asking for knitting wool for their gran, or looking round desperately and settling on a reel of cotton, when clearly all they wanted was to look at Stella.

One of them had given her Bertie. He worked in the grocer's, and he'd been hanging around for weeks. Popping in when he was out delivering. Adding a tin of something nice or a jar of jam to their shopping. Then he'd turned up at the shop with bulging pockets – a tin of corned beef in one, and a puppy in the other. He'd handed both to Stella, who clutched them automatically, and asked her out to the cinema. Molly thought her sister looked like she might say yes, but then Mum had surged up from behind the counter like some kind of warrior queen and told him that if he ever bothered her daughter again she'd have the law on him. He went, but he left the puppy.

Molly hadn't expected that they'd keep the dog – they already had a huge ginger cat, boringly called Tom, and Mum adored him. She wouldn't want a dog as well. She didn't, but then she'd remembered that Burford's had had a window broken the week before, and tools stolen, and that one of her regulars had told her wisely there was a gang out robbing small shops. The puppy was tiny now, but he'd grow. He could see off burglars, and he might help discourage the rats in the yard too.

Bertie didn't actually grow very much. He was

small and whitish and mostly terrier, with a wiry coat and silken ears, but he did have a powerful bark. It was a deep thundering noise that felt as if it belonged to quite another dog, and it seemed to surprise him every time.

Once the evacuation really started, if it ever did, Stella was going to have to be a lot better at looking after him.

"Put the wireless on," Molly's mother added. "If the blackout's starting tomorrow, we'd better listen. Who knows what else that lot have come up with."

Molly turned the set on – it was in the little back sitting room, and it was loud enough that Mum would hear it from the shop.

The announcer was in the middle of a long list of government instructions about the blackout, and appeals for more Air Raid Precaution volunteers. It was quite soothing, twisting her hands to help Stella wind the wool, and listening to the man on the wireless, his voice so polite and calm. There could be bombs dropping on the BBC already,

Molly thought, and he wouldn't stop telling people about information bureaux for the Territorial Army. Then Stella tugged sharply on the wool she was winding, and Molly squeaked.

"Listen!" Stella leaned towards the door, almost pulling the skein of wool from Molly's hands.

"The Ministry of Health today issued the order to evacuate forthwith. Please follow all instructions previously communicated in your local area. This should not be taken to mean that war is now inevitable."

"Forthwith?" Molly met her sister's eyes, both of them looking frightened. They had been waiting for it for so long, but now it was actually going to happen. "Does that mean – now? Have I got to go back to school? I haven't packed properly, my parcel's all coming undone!"

Stella shook her head. "No, tomorrow morning. Early, isn't it? You'd better go and find everything you need."

Molly looked round sharply. Their mother

was standing in the doorway, the knitting still clutched in her hand. The room was darker, with her blocking the light from the shop, and the girls shifted anxiously on the piled-up boxes.

"She needs to go and pack, Mum," Stella said. "I can iron her dress ready for tomorrow. Her pink cotton's clean."

Their mother shook her head and went back into the shop, her voice trailing over her shoulder. "She isn't going."

Molly stood up, her legs suddenly shaky. Not going? Everyone was going. London was going to be *bombed*. Miss had said so. And if it wasn't a bomb that got her, it would be the gas. They had the masks, they'd been practising for ages, even doing lessons with them on. The tops of the letter boxes were painted greeny-yellow with the gas detector paint, so they'd change colour when it was coming.

As soon as war was declared for real, the Germans were going to drop gas and bombs on London, to try to win the war all at once. Everyone knew that. Molly had to go, because she was a child, and children were to be kept safe, even if that meant leaving the not-children behind, where they would be not-safe.

Everyone was going.

Stella followed their mother back into the shop. "Mum, what do you mean? Molly's on the evacuation list. You signed her up. You filled in the forms. You said you did."

"I've changed my mind."

"But — but you can't." Stella shook her head. "You just can't. She's got to go and be safe, Mum."

Molly crept up behind her, winding her hands in Stella's yellow cardigan. Her sister had knitted it herself, and she'd made one for Molly to match. Molly minded about leaving Mum, of course she did. But she minded leaving Stella and Bertie more. Stella didn't hold on to her so tight. Molly could feel Mum clutching at her right now, even though she was half a room away, leaning heavily on the shop counter.

"She's safe here with us!" their mother hissed. "I'm not sending her off to be looked after by strangers! We don't even know where the children are going, and the school doesn't know either. I'm not putting her on a train if I haven't a clue when I'm going to see her again, Stella. She could end up on the other side of the country!"

"Miss said parents can come and visit," Molly put in, her voice husky. She was almost sure it was no use arguing, it never was, but she had to try.

"Much good that is, if you're in – in Wales. And I've a shop to run," her mother pointed out wearily. "I want you here, Molly. Where I can see you."

"They said on the wireless. . ." Stella shook her head, as if she were trying to clear her thoughts. "They said 'Evacuate forthwith', but that it doesn't mean war is inevitable. Mum, if they have to say that – I mean, that's the kind of thing they say to make you feel better. Like pulling a tooth out isn't going to hurt. Of course it is! The war's coming, Mum, it's going to be any day. Molly has to get away from the bombs, she could be killed."

"So could we." Mum stood straight, pushing herself wearily up off the counter. "Don't you see, Stella? Your dad's gone – Molly never even knew him. I've had years without him, years. I'm not being without Molly now. If we go, we all go together. Don't you see?"

Chapter Two

"That's dry."

Molly blinked at the plate she was holding, and stopped rubbing at it with the tea towel. Bertie had been leaning against her foot, and now he stood up and nosed at her, looking hopeful. He was after leftovers, but there hadn't been much to leave.

"You'll take the pattern off it," Stella said, smiling at her. It wasn't very funny, but Molly tried to smile back. She put the plate on the dresser, and picked up the one that Stella had just taken out of the water. Mum cooked, and they washed up, it was the same every night – and it would go on being the same. Everything was going to be the same.

"Things *will* be different," Stella murmured, and Molly looked up, startled. She hadn't spoken aloud. "I know you were looking forward to going to the country."

"All my friends are going," Molly said, trying not to bang the plate down too angrily. "It isn't fair. Mum wants me to get blown up by a bomb – she said so!"

"That's not what she meant. You know that really. She's just – she can't let go, Molly, not since Dad died. She looked after him for so long when his lungs got really bad, always running up and down the stairs from the shop. She just can't bear breaking us all up."

"I'm not staying here when I'm older," Molly said, glaring at her sister. "When I'm as old as you, I'm going to get a job somewhere else. I'm not going to work in the shop." Stella looked sideways at her, and then ducked her head, gazing down into the water. She looked furtive – almost guilty – and Molly leaned closer. "What? What have you done?"

"Nothing!" But Stella had pink patches at the tops of her cheeks. She was definitely lying.

"You have." Molly dipped her hand in the sink and splashed her with the greasy water, so Stella yelped and jumped back. "Tell me! Stella, have you gone and got another job?" There was no reason why Stella couldn't do something different. She could even move out and live on her own, Molly realized suddenly. She was seventeen, after all, not far off eighteen. She could live in a hostel, or rent a room.

"I haven't yet," Stella muttered, flushing even more. "But I'm going to." She looked up and stared determinedly at her little sister. "I'm going to join one of the services. The ATS, probably. I thought of being a Wren, but Pearl next door says it's all posh girls from smart families."

"When did you talk to Pearl?" Molly gaped at her. Mum didn't approve of Pearl at all. She went

21

out to the cinema with a string of lads, and she wore make-up that you could see. Mum said that anything more than a little touch of powder made a girl look cheap.

"In the yard, hanging out the washing. She wants to join the WAAF but I don't think I'd care for it." Stella shook her head. "Pearl says the girls wouldn't ever have to fly, but still. It makes me feel queasy."

"What do the ATS do?" Molly asked. "How do you even know about them, anyway?" She was asking questions to stop the sinking feeling inside her. Stella was going away. Stella was going, instead of her. It would be just Molly and Mum, all the time. She crouched down and put her arms round Bertie, and he licked her face delightedly.

"It's always on the wireless, isn't it? And I read that book that came through the door." Stella rubbed briskly at the plates with a dishcloth. "The National Service Handbook. The WAAF wasn't even in that, it's too new. Pearl likes new things."

"New boyfriend every week," Molly muttered.

It was what Mum said. Molly hadn't even had to think, it just came out of her mouth. Actually, Molly liked Pearl. She always said hello, and she'd given Molly a choc once, out of a proper box with puppies on the lid.

"Don't be a little cat. Anyway. The ATS is the army for girls. And I don't know what I'd be doing, it could be anything." Stella looked out of the window into the yard, her hands in the water. "They might even teach me to drive. Can you imagine, me driving a car, Molly?" Then she sighed. "Or it could be washing up, just like here. Except it won't be here, don't you see?"

Molly nodded. She absolutely did.

"I'm going to do it tomorrow."

Molly wobbled a little as Bertie pulled away from her, and she watched as he went nosing and wagging towards the kitchen door. The half-open kitchen door.

"Stella. . ." she whispered, and her sister swung round, her eyes widening.

"You won't," their mother said, pushing the door properly open. She ignored the dog. "I won't let you."

Molly waited for her sister to bow her head, and nod, and finish the washing up, the way she always did. But Stella braced herself against the sink and picked up the tea towel that Molly had left on the side. She began to dry her hands, very slowly, a finger at a time. "You don't have to let me," she said calmly. "You can't stop me."

Molly watched her, and realized that Stella was drying her hands with the tea towel to cover up that they were shaking. Her mum could probably see too – but it was making Stella feel stronger, to pretend that she wasn't scared.

"I'm your mother. You're only seventeen."

"I'll be eighteen in a month." Stella twisted the tea towel between her hands, and looked clearly at her mother. "How are you going to stop me then?"

"If you do this..." Their mother's eyes darted

sideways as she tried to think of a threat. "I won't let you stay here. I'll throw you out."

Stella shrugged. "The ATS has barracks, like the army do. I'll be living there anyway."

Molly couldn't help it. She caught at Stella's yellow sleeve, gazing up at her pleadingly. Stella put her own hand over Molly's fingers, and Molly could feel her trembling now.

Their mother smiled. "You won't see her. If you go, that means you don't come back. You'd better say goodbye to her, hadn't you?"

"How can you be like this?" Stella suddenly exploded. "You went to that same ARP meeting about the air raids and gas that I did. Haven't you listened to the wireless? Don't you care about the war effort at all?"

"No." Mum shook her head. "No. The last war killed your father, even if it did take him fifteen years to die from the gas. I'm not taking any part in this one. And Molly's staying here with me."

Stella's shoulders sagged. "It's not like that!

Mum, they're going to drop bombs on us. You can't just say you're not having it. It isn't up to you whether you want to join in." She lifted her hand away from Molly's and walked around the table to take hold of her mother's arms. "We've all got gas masks, Mum. Why do you think that is? They're going to drop the same stuff all over again, the gas that poisoned Dad."

"Don't say things like that!"

Molly watched as Stella shook her. She did it only gently, but their mother was limp, like a doll – and then she leaned on Stella's shoulder, and Molly could hear her crying quietly into the yellow cardigan.

Bertie woke Molly the next morning by licking her cheek. She spluttered, and sighed, and put her hand gently over his nose to push him away. He wasn't really meant to sleep on the bed but last night had been still too full of tears and shouting and more tears and regretful hugs. Neither Stella nor Mum had the energy to make her take him back downstairs. Molly glanced across at the other side of the bed – Stella was still asleep. It was early, but the room was already light enough to see. In the other houses in their road, children would be getting up, taking their gas masks and bundles of clothes, and eating a last slice of bread and marge at home before they left.

"Do you need to go out?" she whispered to him, and Bertie whisked his tail and licked her again and whined.

Molly wriggled out of bed, shushing the dog, and dragged on her dress and cardigan. Then, holding Bertie by the collar so that he didn't bark and dance about, she crept downstairs. There was the end of a loaf in the bread bin, so she sawed off a thick slice, grabbed her gas mask from the hook in the hall and slipped out into the street. Bertie followed her, eyeing the bread hopefully. Molly tore pieces off as she walked, half for her and half for Bertie. They had finished it by the time they got to the end of the street, and she was still hungry. "It's all gone," she told Bertie, showing him her hands, but he stared at her with huge, disbelieving eyes. "We'll get something else when we go back home," she murmured. "Soon, I promise."

As they turned the corner into the main road, Molly saw a slow stream of children making for the school. They were quieter than usual, and most of them had family with them even if they usually walked on their own. Now there were worried-looking mothers and fathers carrying parcels or cases. One of the girls from Molly's class turned back to stare at her in surprise – it was obvious that she wasn't going with them, with no coat or bag, and a small dog following next to her.

"Aren't you coming?" Elsie shouted across the road.

Molly shook her head. "My mum says no," she called back, her fingers tightening on Bertie's lead. "She wants me at home."

Elsie's mother shook her head disapprovingly, and hurried Elsie and her little sister on.

Molly kept walking, pressing herself and Bertie in towards the side of the pavement when hurrying families came past. The school gates were surrounded by a crowd of mothers, and Molly's teacher was writing names on a list as the children came in. Molly stopped by the railings, watching as the staff marshalled children into lines, and the caretaker stood waiting, holding a placard printed with "Hanley Road School". Elsie was standing there talking excitedly to Sally and Jean, while her little sister clung grimly on to a battered-looking knitted bear. A few children had cases, or canvas kitbags, but most of them were holding pillowcases or paper parcels.

Sally broke out of the line and dashed across to the railings, with Jean following after her. They both had labels tied around the top buttons of their coats, luggage labels neatly lettered with their names as though they were parcels being sent off on a train. "What's going on? Elsie says you're not coming, but you are, aren't you? You're on Miss's list."

"My mum changed her mind. She said. . ." Molly trailed off. She couldn't really repeat what Mum had said about dying together to Sally and Jean. Not when they were about to leave their parents behind. "She said she didn't want me to go to strangers."

"You two, get yourselves back in the line, we're leaving in a minute." One of the teachers came bustling over. "Molly Mason, what are you doing out there?"

"Just saying goodbye, miss."

"You aren't coming?"

"My mum says I'm not allowed."

The teacher frowned at her. "Well, you'd better get off home then, dear. We're about to go."

"Yes, miss." Molly didn't, though. She backed away a little, and waited until the teacher had hurried off to sort out a squabble among a bunch of Infants, then she stood close against the wall and watched.

Bertie whined next to her, but she shushed

him, even though she knew he was right. Mum and Stella would be looking for her, or at least, she hoped they would. Perhaps they hadn't noticed that she was gone? Perhaps she could just go up to Miss, and add her name to that list, and go away to the countryside after all, instead of being left behind.

Except that she had Bertie with her, and no little case. Molly sighed as the caretaker marched out of the gates, and a slow, straggling column of children followed him, shooed along by teachers. The mothers, and a few fathers, surged behind them, waving and calling, and blocking Molly's view. She couldn't see Sally and Jean, they were lost in the crowd. She dodged around the knot of parents, and scurried ahead on the other side of the road, standing in a shop doorway to watch as the caretaker led the way with his placard. The file of children marched behind, each with a luggage label tied on to one of their coat buttons. Sally was crying again, Molly noticed as she waved and waved, and so was Pete, and their mum. Jean was giving Sally a handkerchief, and she didn't look across the road, even though Molly called. They'd left her behind already.

Stella eyed Molly worriedly as she crept back in. "What's the matter? Where *did* you disappear off to, this early?"

"School," Molly muttered. "To see everyone going off to the country. Where are you going?" she added accusingly, noting that Stella had her good jacket on.

"To join up for the ATS."

"I don't believe it! She's letting you?"

Stella lifted the kettle off the gas and poured boiling water into the teapot. "It's like I said. She can't stop me going, can she?"

"But what about me?"

"She didn't mean it about me not being allowed to come back. She was just – shouting. You know what she's like."

Molly sniffed. "Of course I do. And now you're going and I'm not. It'll be just me and Mum. I can't even go to school!"

Stella blinked at her. "What do you mean?"

"My school isn't there," Molly hissed crossly. "They've all gone, haven't they? All the teachers, and nearly all my class. School's going to be in – wherever they are."

"There isn't anywhere else for you to go?"

"I don't know. No one said. If you're not here I'll just have to help Mum in the shop all the time." Molly glanced miserably at the storeroom and the shop beyond, all the shelves and shelves she'd be stuck with tidying and dusting and counting.

"That can't be right," Stella muttered. "Lots of people haven't sent their kids, I'm sure of it. Mrs Dance was telling me in the baker's that she's keeping hers home." She glanced up at the clock. "I'd better go. I'll be back later this morning, I should think." She picked up her hat from the table and pinned it on, tucking her curls this way and that, and humming to herself in the little mirror, while Molly watched resentfully. Stella looked so happy.

"You will come back, won't you?" Molly asked suddenly, as Stella let herself out of the back door. "They won't send you away right now?"

"Of course they won't," said Stella as she kissed her cheek, laughing. "I'm only filling in papers, Molly, I promise."

She pulled the door sharply shut behind her, and Molly looked down at Bertie. The little terrier was wagging his tail hopefully, expecting a bit more than half a slice of bread for breakfast.

"At least I don't have to leave you behind now," Molly said, sighing. "You or Stella. And Mum too, I suppose." She *would* have missed her mother. Maybe more than she'd like to admit.

Molly was on her way back from running errands for her mum, and the basket of shopping was heavy. The handle was wearing red marks into her hands, even though she kept swapping it over. She was tired and fed up and she only wanted to get home, so she almost didn't stop when she saw the van outside school. But it tugged at her. School was meant to be all closed up.

Stella had said that there were lots of other children who hadn't gone – and someone in the shop had told her about empty buses waiting for children who didn't turn up – but everywhere still felt lonely and strange. She couldn't run round the corner to knock for Jean or Sally. She didn't even know where they were. Sally's mum had been in the grocer's and she'd told Molly that all the children had been given a postcard to send home with their new address on. But they wouldn't have had time to send them the day before, Molly supposed. There was also no post on Sundays . . . so that would mean three whole days when Sally's mum didn't know where Sally and Pete were.

All of that went through her mind when she saw the van and the little knot of people outside the school. What were they doing? Molly had assumed that the school would just be left locked up and empty. Perhaps some teachers were coming back, for the children who had stayed behind. They couldn't really leave all those children running wild, could they? Forgetting how heavy the basket was, she hurried up closer, hoping to hear what they were saying and maybe get a look inside the van. She wondered if it was full of books – she knew that Miss had said they'd take school books with them, so it made sense someone would need to send more.

"Out of the way, missy." Molly skipped back as two men in overalls came hurrying past, one at each end of a pile of . . . planks of wood? Except that wasn't quite right. What they were carrying was flat and brownish like planks, but it wasn't wood. Molly watched them walk in through the doors of the school. Another man and a woman followed them into the playground and stood there, talking and marking off lists. No one was looking at her. Leaving the basket by the gate, she went to look into the van. There were more of the flat brown packages piled up inside, and – even more strangely – bolts of material. Flowered cottons, mostly. Molly gave them a knowledgeable once-over, and decided that they wouldn't sell well. Some of them looked a bit faded, and the patterns weren't modern.

"Hop it, you."

Molly squeaked and jumped aside. She'd been too busy eyeing the fabric, and not noticed the men coming back.

"No need to be like that, Fred. Off you go, missy. Nothing for you here."

But the kinder of the two men was smiling at her as he said it, and Molly plucked up the courage to speak. "What are those? And why've you got all that material?" Then she had a worried thought. "Are you selling it? There's already a haberdasher's here, you know. My mum keeps it."

The man who'd told her to hop it snorted with

laughter, and pulled another pile of the brown pieces out of the van. It was cardboard, Molly realized, as she saw how light it was to lift. Great piles of cardboard boxes. She supposed they could be for packing the fabric, but it seemed odd. Boxes would usually come full of things, not flat like that.

"They're coffins, Miss Nosy. Cardboard coffins. For when the bombing starts, and there's too many dead to make wooden ones in time." The man smirked at her, but his mate rolled his eyes.

"So much for not causing a panic. Don't you worry, love. This is only for an emergency. Just in case, see? The school's going to be an emergency mortuary."

Molly gaped at him. She couldn't say anything. There were so many of those flat boxes. So many. She'd not heard the word mortuary before, but it was clear that the men meant it was a place for dead people. "What's the fabric for?" she called at last, as the two men carried their load through the gate. But she didn't shout loud enough, and they didn't answer her.

She thought she knew anyway. It was probably to make shrouds to wrap the bodies in. Wartime was not a time to waste things; all the wireless broadcasts kept saying that. Everyone must do their bit, and save the nation's resources. And anyway, if she was dead she wouldn't even know she'd been laid to rest covered in a nasty flowered print.

Chapter Three

This is London. You will now hear a statement from the prime minister.

I am speaking to you from the Cabinet Room at 10 Downing Street. This morning the British Ambassador in Berlin handed the German government a final note stating that, unless we heard from them by eleven o'clock that they were prepared at once to withdraw their troops from Poland, a state of war would exist between us.

I have to tell you now that no such undertaking has been received, and that consequently this *country is at war with Germany.*

Molly pushed her cold hand into Stella's, and watched Mum's fingers tighten on Tom's fur. The ginger cat shifted uncomfortably, and then dug his claws into her mother's skirt and yowled. She let go of him, staring down in shock as Tom shot out of the room.

"Oh..." Mum blinked, and brushed at the pulled threads on her skirt, as though she didn't understand what had happened.

Molly could just hear the thud of paws as Tom landed on the draining board. He was making for the kitchen window, brush-tailed and furious.

Bertie was sitting on Molly's feet, which was good, because she felt cold all over. The prime minister sounded old and sad and broken. It was actually happening. Almost to the last minute, she hadn't been sure. People had been in and out of the shop all week, saying there was still hope, and Mr Chamberlain wouldn't let it happen. But then others said that Hitler had been aiming for a war all along, and it would certainly start any day now. Of course both of those couldn't be right.

The tiny store of hope inside her – which had persisted even after the evacuation, since after all, they could always bring everyone back, couldn't they? – had been dampened down watching the cardboard being carried into school. It was all so worryingly ready. Someone just had to unfold the coffins when it all started.

Molly hadn't told Mum or Stella what she'd seen. Mum seemed still to be pretending that the war was going to pass them by, and Stella was so excited about the new life that she was going to start. She was waiting for a letter, telling her where to report for her training. She seemed brighter and happier already, as if she were starting to break away from their mother's suffocating grip. Molly was trying to be happy for her too, but all the new things that were going to happen to Stella kept reminding her that she was staying at home.

Please stand by for the important government announcements, which as the prime minister has said, will follow almost immediately. That is the end of the announcement.

Bells rang out, and Molly's attention jumped back to the wireless.

This is London. The government have given instructions for the following important announcements.

Closing of places of entertainment: all cinemas, theatres and other places of entertainment are to be closed immediately until further notice. . . They are being closed because if they were hit by a bomb, large numbers would be killed or injured. . .

Air raid warnings: as from now no hooter or siren may be sounded, except on the instructions of the police. In the event of threatened air raids, warnings will be given in urban areas by means of sirens or hooters, which will be sounded in some places by short intermittent blasts and in other places by a warbling note changing every few seconds.

The warning may also be given by short blasts on police whistles. When you hear any of these sounds, take shelter. Do not leave your shelter until you hear the Raiders Passed signal. . .

If poison gas has been used, you will be warned by means of hand rattles. If you hear hand rattles, do not leave your shelter until the poison gas has been cleared away.

There was a scuffling noise. They had been sitting so intensely still that it seemed very loud to Molly, but it was only Stella getting up and going to crouch by their mum's chair and hold her hand. Mum didn't say anything – it was as if she didn't even notice Stella. But the skin on her face looked pale and damp, like an expensive wax doll.

Handbells will be used to tell you when there is no longer any danger from poison gas.

Schools: all day schools in evacuation and neutral areas in England, Wales and Scotland are to be closed for lessons for at least a week from today. . . Molly glanced across at Stella, about to say

I told you so, but Stella was still clinging to Mum and gazing fixedly at the wireless, her face drained of colour. The words died away in Molly's mouth.

General: keep off the streets as much as possible. To expose yourself unnecessarily adds to your danger. Carry your gas mask with you always. Make sure that you and every member of your household, especially children able to run about, have on them their names and address clearly written... Sew the label on to your children's clothes, where they cannot pull it off.

Why? Molly wondered. Her thoughts were jumping and jittering about. No school for a week? Did that mean school would be starting again after that? But her school was full of coffins now. No cinema to go to. That had been their treat. What did a warbling note sound like? Was it like a bird singing? And *why* must she have a label sewn into her clothes?

"God Save the King" began to play on the wireless, and Molly twitched. She should stand up – they always had to when the national anthem played at school, it was the right thing to do. But Mum and Stella were still curled against each other, not moving. Molly stood up uncertainly, and Bertie stood too, wagging his tail slowly from side to side and gazing at her. Then he stiffened, and Molly saw the wiry hairs rise up along the length of his back. His teeth showed, just a little, white points gleaming as his muzzle wrinkled back.

"Bertie?" Molly whispered, and then a dreadful shrieking wail broke out, rising and falling, like how Bertie himself howled when he was shut in.

"Is that it?" Molly gasped, crouching down to put her arms around him as he growled. "Is that the siren? Is it a raid?"

"It must be. Oh my God." Stella stumbled up, looking around wildly. "Mum! We have to go. We've got to get down the road."

There was no space for one of the metal Anderson shelters in their yard, brick-paved as it was, but council workmen had built a massive version at the end of the street. An arch of corrugated iron, piled up over the sides and roof with sandbags. Molly had peeped into it once – there were benches all round the sides and a few oil lamps, but that was all.

"Molly, get the gas masks." Stella pulled their mother up out of her chair. "Mum, come on."

Molly raced into the kitchen to grab the three gas masks in their cardboard boxes, and then followed Molly and Mum out through the shop. All along the street, people were emerging from the shops and houses, looking terrified. The noise of the siren echoed above them, so loud that Molly was sure she could see it moving in the air. Bertie was pressed against her legs, still growling low in his throat.

Their mum suddenly seemed to wake up as she came out into the street, patting at her hair to see if it was tidy. But then she froze on the front step, looking around. "What about Tom? We should have put him in a basket. Where is he?"

"He went out of the kitchen window," Molly said, pulling the door shut behind them and locking it with the key Stella passed her.

Mum reached back to take the key, obviously wanting to go back and call for Tom, but then a young man in a dark boiler suit and a tin hat came running down the street, shouting and twirling a wooden rattle above his head. "Take cover! Take cover! Get to the shelters!"

Molly pushed Stella sharply. "That means there's gas. That's what they just said on the wireless, a rattle means gas and they'll ring a handbell when it's gone. Stella, run!" She grabbed Bertie's collar – she hadn't thought to snatch up his lead – and pulled him with her along the street, with Stella hurrying Mum after her.

There was already a stream of people disappearing into the sandbagged building, with another man in a boiler suit at the door, taking names. As they got closer he shook his head at

Bertie. "No dogs."

"But – but what do I do with him?" Molly asked helplessly.

"There's not room, love," the man said, and Molly realized that he was the tobacconist who sold her sweets. He looked different under the tin hat.

"Oh, let her have her dog, Jack," someone called from inside. "Peggy's got her budgerigar. He's only a little thing."

"Just this once," Mr Timmins muttered, "since there isn't time to argue. And if he causes a nuisance, he's out, mind?"

"He'll be good," Molly promised hurriedly, scooting into the stale-smelling dimness. Bertie followed her, snuffling.

"Is there gas?" Stella asked their neighbours as they settled on to a bench. "One of the ARP workers was sounding a rattle, but I couldn't see anything. Would we even see it?" she added anxiously. "Is it like a cloud?"

"That was Alfie Harker losing his head,"

Mr Timmins called back from the door. "Got overexcited and started waving that rattle about. No gas as far as we know."

"Ohhh. . ." Stella sighed, and leaned back against the wall. "Did you hear that, Mum?" she added gently. "It's all right. No gas."

"I'm going back." Their mum stood up and started to blunder towards the door, still half-open as more people hurried in. "We'd be better at home, it's safer there. And I have to find the cat."

"No!" Stella yelped, hauling her back, and several voices joined in.

"Don't get into a state."

"Sit down, Mrs Mason. Cats have nine lives, he'll be tucked away somewhere safe."

"Have a biscuit, love. I brought a bag of those broken ones from Woolworths. Best to be prepared."

Molly felt Bertie wriggle eagerly as he heard the crumbly rustle of the paper bag of biscuits, and when the bag was passed along, she took a couple of pieces and slipped them to him. She couldn't risk him making a fuss and getting thrown out among the bombs. "When will the planes come?" she whispered to Stella. "I can't hear them."

"We're safe here, dear," the lady with the biscuits murmured, reaching out and patting her knee. "Just sit tight."

They waited tensely, whispering every so often, but everyone was trying to listen for the sound of aircraft, or even bombs dropping. Molly wished she knew what they were supposed to sound like. It would be better to know what to expect.

"We should have sent Molly away," Stella whispered shakily. "When are they going to come? This waiting – it's cruel."

Molly leaned against Stella's shoulder, and pushed her hand into her sister's. Then she blinked as the door opened again and the light rushed in. Another ARP worker was standing at the door, talking to Mr Timmins – and then the siren blared again, one long droning note this time.

"All clear?" one of the men sitting further in asked. "But nothing happened. Did they miss us? Where did they hit?" Everyone began to make for the door, hurrying outside and gazing around anxiously. Once outside, Molly turned a slow circle in the street. There was no bomb damage. The greenish-yellow paint on top of the postbox hadn't changed colour. Molly was almost disappointed. This was war, and everything still looked the same.

Monday should have been the first proper day back at school after the summer holidays. Instead there had been that strange week of waiting – and now there was nothing. Molly's mother had expected the school to reopen as usual, even though Molly had assured her the building was closed. In the end she had marched Molly down there, leaving Stella to mind the shop. The school was locked up, and there was a sign on the gates saying that it was closed until further notice. There was nothing about the emergency mortuary, but Molly supposed people weren't meant to know until the emergency had happened. Parents of children still in evacuation areas should enquire at the council offices, the sign said. But Molly's mother read it and sniffed, and pointed out that she didn't have time for that now, she had a shop to run. Molly had better just come home, she said irritably. She could help out at the shop until they knew what was happening. Molly had already spent all the summer holiday helping out – when she wasn't sneaking away to find Sally and Jean whenever she could. She followed her mum back home feeling dismal.

She had never been able to spend that much time with Sally and Jean, not with helping in the shop and running errands or hanging out the washing or whatever else it was Mum wanted her to do. Sometimes she felt left out when the other two chattered on about things she'd missed. Now she was missing *everything*. Sally and Jean were halfway to Wales, or that was what Jean's mother had told Mum when they met her in the street, grumbling about how far away it was. Some tiny village, apparently. Billeting Molly's school there had practically doubled the population. She wondered whether they were doing lessons in a strange school building, all squashed in.

Molly's mother sent her out to do the shopping when they got back, with a list of all the everyday things, and another list of odds and ends that Mum and Stella had heard through local gossip would run short before long. Hairpins were the most important thing – Stella wanted at least six packets. There had already been several elderly women in the shop buying up knicker elastic and buttons. All the sorts of small, not really important but vital things that had been very hard to get hold of in the last war.

It was when Molly was walking down to the pharmacist for a bottle of Vicks cough syrup – her mum swore by it, and had suddenly thought that perhaps they'd better lay up a stock – that she saw the line. The pharmacy was off the main street, close by the clinic, and there was a vet's in the same road. Molly had been there before to buy a box of vitamin powders to sprinkle on Bertie's food, because she and Stella had been worried that the little dog didn't seem to be getting any bigger. The powders hadn't made a lot of difference, though.

Molly had never seen a queue that came out of the surgery itself. When she went to buy the vitamin powders there had been just a small girl with an enormous rabbit in her arms waiting to see the vet, and two dogs, and that was it. Now there were people all along the pavement, waiting with dogs on leads or cats shut up in baskets. Every so often there would be an outbreak of furious hissing as one of the dogs came too close – Molly saw one ferocious paw shoot out under the lid of a basket, and the unlucky dog darted back around its owner's ankles.

Perhaps they were all there for something like those Admin powders she had bought, Molly wondered to herself. It said on the advertisements that they were good for nervous dogs, as well as helping puppies to grow. The sirens had probably sent an awful lot of dogs and cats into a panic. Bertie hadn't seemed too upset, but Molly was sure he had known the siren was going to sound before it began. If dogs could tell that a raid was about to happen, it made sense that they would be scared. But if all these people only wanted vitamin powders, why would they need to bring their dogs with them? And were there even vitamins for cats? If there were, Molly had never seen them – and the way Mum fussed over Tom, she would definitely have bought them for him.

Curiously, Molly wandered past the line of people, admiring the dogs and peeking into the cat baskets. A little terrier with fawn-spotted ears like Bertie's jumped up at her shopping basket as she walked by, and the woman holding his lead apologized, pulling him back. "I'm sorry. He's a bit jumpy, waiting with all these other people. I think the cats are getting to him!" She gave a little laugh, but she sounded anxious, and Molly smiled at her.

"It doesn't matter. He's beautiful, he looks like my dog. What's his name?"

"Perkins," the woman answered, but she didn't smile, or agree that he was lovely, the way Molly had expected. Usually if she admired a dog that was out with its owner, they were glad to talk about how clever their pet was, or how naughty. Instead the woman pulled the little dog close, and turned away from Molly as though she'd said something rude.

Molly almost walked on, but then the woman reached down and picked Perkins up, snuggling him against her dress, and Molly saw that she was crying.

"I'm sorry," she said hurriedly. "Is he ill? I didn't mean to make you cry, I'm ever so sorry."

The woman made a strange, gulping, wailing noise, and the teenage boy ahead of her in the line glared at Molly. "Haven't you got any sense?" he muttered. "What did you have to make it worse for?"

Molly blinked at him. From the way he was

talking, she was meant to know what was going on, and she just didn't. "I only asked," she whispered crossly. "I wasn't trying to make anything worse. What's wrong with her dog?"

The boy glared back at her, and the wicker basket in his arms creaked. There was a little black cat inside, shifting around nervously. Molly could see its golden eyes glinting. The cat was glaring at her too. It looked perfectly healthy, as far as she could see. Just a bit cross. But then there didn't seem to be anything the matter with Perkins, either, except that he wanted to eat the mince in Molly's shopping basket. All the dogs in the line looked quite bright and cheerful, though it was harder to tell with the cats.

"There's going to be food shortages," the boy muttered. "Nothing to feed them on. And the bombs – they might send the dogs wild. Because of the noise, you know. So. . ." He shrugged, and lifted the basket a little higher and closer, so that the cat inside shifted again and let out a fretful mew.

Molly's stomach turned over. There wasn't anything wrong with the dogs or cats at all. Every single animal in that line was perfectly healthy.

She didn't go on past the front of the line to the pharmacy. If Mum made a fuss, she'd just say they'd not had any Vicks. She needed to get back home now, this minute.

All the people waiting in the street were quiet, Molly realized, as she hurried past them again. Hardly anyone was chatting. The boy with the black cat was staring after her resentfully, as though it was Molly's fault he was there. The lady who owned Perkins was patting her eyes with a handkerchief. It was quite clear that she didn't want to be waiting for the vet, but she was going to do it anyway. She was going to have that greedy, darling little terrier put down, because who knew what was going to happen tomorrow. A dog or a cat was just another thing to worry about in the panic of saying goodbye to the children and getting the blackout ready.

There was too much to worry about.

As she reached the corner of the street, Molly broke into a run. Perkins had soft, silky brownish ears, just like Bertie. She had to get home.

Bertie tried to eat the mince, too, when Molly dumped the basket on the kitchen floor and went to hug him. He was far more interested in the shopping than he was in her, but he let Molly put her arms around him and gave her cheek a quick lick before he went back to sniffing the basket.

"Don't let that dog in the shopping, Molly, don't you have any sense?" said Molly's mother as she grabbed hold of the basket and lifted it on to the table away from Bertie. "Whatever's the matter? You're scarlet in the face."

"Nothing. . ." Molly let go of Bertie, who was wriggling madly, and stood up, eyeing her mother cautiously. Had Mum heard what people were doing? No one had mentioned it in the shop, or not in front of Molly, anyway. She didn't want to ask, in case it gave Mum ideas.

There was a scuffling noise, and Tom appeared at the kitchen window. He stepped cautiously around the plates drying in the rack, and jumped over to the kitchen table, rubbing the side of his head against Molly's mum's sleeve and purring throatily at her.

Molly watched her mum smile delightedly – Tom wasn't always so affectionate. Mum ran her hand over his ears and scratched him under the chin, murmuring to him about how beautiful he was. Then she drew her hand away and glanced at Molly. "Did you get that tin of sardines I sent you for?" she asked.

Molly nodded and went to dig around in the basket for it. She started to put the rest of the shopping away in the larder and the meat safe, while Mum fetched a cracked china dish they often used to feed Tom, and opened the tin with the little key on top. Tom could obviously smell the fish as soon as the tin began to open, he was purring like an engine and he kept nudging Mum's arm, so she almost spilled the sardine oil everywhere. "Give over, you silly creature," she murmured, but she didn't tell him off. She didn't put the dish down on the floor when she'd mashed up the sardines, either. She let Tom gulp them down crouched on the kitchen table, and she watched him until he'd licked the last gleam of oil off the dish. Then he sat on the table smugly washing his whiskers and eyeing Bertie, who was curled up on his blanket looking envious and wistful.

Mum put the dish in the sink, then she wheeled round and marched back to the shop without a word.

Molly stood in the middle of the kitchen gazing after her and looked back at the empty dish. A whole tin of sardines to himself, in the middle of the day, and on the kitchen table? Any other day, Tom might get a little spoonful, and then only if they were having sardines on toast for tea.

"I wouldn't look so pleased with yourself," Molly whispered shakily to the cat. "I really wouldn't."

Tom looked at her and lazily swept one big paw over his ears. He didn't seem worried, but Molly felt cold all over.

The shop was busy – lots of people seemed to be trying to stock up, the way Stella had with hairpins – and Molly was sent dashing backwards and forwards to the stockroom or out to the kitchen to make cups of tea. There was no chance for her to talk to Stella about what she suspected. Instead, she spent the whole day watching their mother out of the corner of her eye. Did Mum always make such a fuss of Tom? Was she frowning like that because she felt guilty, and worried, or was she just annoyed with Mrs Barrett asking for six different shades of sewing thread that they didn't have? It was so hard to tell. If it hadn't been for the sardines, Molly would have thought she was imagining it, but Mum would never usually spoil Tom that much.

"I'll have to go up to those council offices and

ask about school for Molly tomorrow," her mother said as they were eating tea. "You might have to go a bit further away." She chewed thoughtfully for a moment, and then shook her head. "But then they said not to be out on the streets when you didn't need to! It doesn't make sense, it really doesn't."

Molly didn't say, *You should have let me go with the others*. If she'd gone away to the country, there would be no one to look out for Bertie and Tom. If only she knew for certain what Mum was planning to do. Perhaps she was imagining Mum being extra nice to Tom? Perhaps Mum just wanted to give him a treat, to make up for the way she'd grabbed on to him too tightly during the prime minister's broadcast the day before? Molly reached under the table and slipped Bertie a crust of bread and potted meat. She was probably worrying for nothing. Wouldn't her mum be more worried if she was planning on having Tom and Bertie put down? She wouldn't be spending time fussing about schools.

Stella and Molly went to wash the plates as

usual, but then Mum called from the shop. "Stella! I need a hand with this, love. Come and help me reach the top shelves."

Molly was so jumpy she nearly dropped the cup she was drying, but Stella didn't notice. "I'll be back in a minute. Just put those plates in to soak."

Molly put the cup down, her fingers trembling, and crept across the kitchen to the door. She couldn't hear what Mum and Stella were saying – the door between the stockroom and the shop was closed. Bertie was creeping after her, his tail wagging. He could sense that something was happening – perhaps the same way he'd known the siren was about to howl, Molly thought.

She edged the door open just a tiny crack, trying to listen. Mum and Stella weren't putting anything on shelves, she was sure. They were standing by the counter, both of them.

"But I don't see why. . ." Stella was saying, her voice worried.

"Look!" Molly heard a rustle of paper.

She pressed herself right up against the door, wishing she could hear better. She couldn't see what it was that Mum had passed Stella at all.

"It was in this morning's paper again," Mum murmured. "Air Raid Precautions for Animals. It's all very well saying send them to someone in the country, but do they think we're made of money? And who am I supposed to ask to take them? We don't know anyone."

Molly heard Stella laugh. "You could hardly tell everyone you evacuated the dog and the cat but not your daughter, could you?"

"Don't be like that about it," Mum snapped back. "You know why I wanted her here. What are we going to do?"

Stella was silent for a moment. "What do you mean?" she said at last.

There was a sigh. "Look what it says at the bottom of the page. 'If you cannot place them in the care of neighbours, it really is kindest to have them destroyed.'"

"That can't be right." The paper rustled again, and then there was quiet – Stella must have been reading the article for herself.

Molly held her breath. Bertie was Stella's, officially, even if Molly looked after him most of the time. Stella wouldn't let him be destroyed.

"You're not going to do it, are you?" Stella said at last. "I know you don't like the puppy much, Mum, but Tom! We've had him years. You couldn't. . ."

"There won't be any food for him," their mother muttered. "I don't want him starving and terrified when the bombing starts. They say it's for the best. The kindest thing to do. Mrs Banks showed me an ARP booklet for animal owners this morning when she came in for buttons – that's what it said, that it was cruel to make them suffer. There was an advertisement for a bolt pistol in it."

"I'm not going to shoot the dog, Mum!"

Molly leaned back against the wall, staring down at Bertie. His tail was flickering. He could tell there was something going on, and he was puzzled. He glanced around the edge of the door, his stubby whiskers twitching as he tried to nudge it open. Molly pulled him back quickly.

"I'm not saying we should do it ourselves. You can take them to the vet in Salisbury Street."

"I'm not doing it."

Behind the door, Molly shook her head. That wasn't what Stella was supposed to say. She was supposed to say no, never, we're keeping them, how could you even think of doing something so cruel. But she didn't. There was a shifting, uncomfortable silence on the other side of the door, and then Molly's mother said, "You can take them in the morning when I'm going to the council about the school. I'll take Molly with me. We'll say the shop's closed due to, I don't know, unforeseen circumstances."

"I can't, Mum. Come on. It isn't as if either of them eat that much. Tom catches his own, most of the time, he only has the odd skewer from the cats' meat man. And Bertie has liver and lights from the butcher."

"That'll be what we're all eating before long, you wait and see," her mother said grimly. "And it isn't the food that's worrying me, anyhow, it's the danger. Who knows what that dog will do when the bombs start falling? You're the one who's off to join the forces, Stella, telling me it's all about the war effort and doing your bit! It's not right, keeping them. It's not patriotic."

"But what are you going to say to Molly?" Stella murmured. "She loves Bertie, and all her friends are gone now, she doesn't have anyone to play with. He's company for her. Like Tom's company for you, Mum."

"Nonsense. He's only here to keep down the mice."

"You know that isn't true! You'd miss him. And I won't be here, Mum. You'll be lonely."

"I'll have Molly, and there's the shop. I'll be run off my feet without you here. I won't have time for fussing over a cat, let alone the dog as well. You can take them tomorrow. There's a basket for Tom in the cupboard under the stairs, I'll look it out. And we'll tell Molly that we've sent them to friends in the country, just like it says to in the paper."

There were footsteps then, and Molly darted back through the stockroom and into the kitchen, sloshing water over the plates and frantically scrubbing at the teacup she'd abandoned on the table. "What did Mum want?" she asked, trying to sound as if it wasn't really that important.

"Nothing," Stella said, after an uncomfortable pause. "There was a display card of – of darning needles she wanted reached down, that's all. And then we thought there might have been a mouse running along the back of the shelf. But there wasn't."

Chapter Four

Today. Stella was going to take Bertie to the vet this morning; it was all arranged.

Molly lay on her side of the bed, staring up at the ceiling, or where she knew the ceiling was. She'd peered out round the new blind, and it was only just starting to get light outside, but the room was thickly black still. She had helped Mum stick black paper borders round the glass, so that no cracks of light could escape, and there was a cone of more black paper around the ceiling bulb.

Stella was still fast asleep, snuffling softly into

her pillow. Their mum would be asleep too, in the room across the landing. They were both good sleepers, tired out from being on their feet all day in the shop.

There was no point going in the middle of the night, Molly had decided. A little girl and a dog, traipsing across London in the dark? Someone was bound to stop her. But in the early morning, that was different. So she'd let herself go to sleep. Or she'd tried to, at any rate. She'd lain there next to Stella for what felt like hours, thinking of more and more things that might go wrong with her plan. Molly curled up against her, sniffing the violet stuff that she put on her hair, and thought how much she hated it, she always had. She wished that she could just kick her sister awake and tell her she mustn't do what Mum said.

But it wouldn't work. Stella was different now, Molly was sure, even though it had only been the war for a day and a half. She had gone off to join up when Mum had said she mustn't, and somehow she had got away with it. Stella wasn't going to risk upsetting Mum over Bertie and Tom, not when she was winning her own private battle. She was letting them go. And *she* was the one *taking* them.

Molly had put her hairbrush in the bed with her, so that even if she fell properly asleep, she'd roll over on it and wake up. That was the plan. Instead she half-dozed and kept jerking awake, lying there listening out for the clock on the church at the end of the road. The bells weren't allowed any more, but the clock still rang the hours. It had rung four o'clock just a little while before.

So if she was going, she'd better go now.

She had spent the whole evening on a stool in the corner of the sitting room, helping her mother darn stockings and listening to the organ music on the wireless. After that there were yet more announcements about ARP, and gas masks, and labelling your children Stella had sewn a label inside Molly's coat, a cloth one, written in marking ink. She and Mum had agreed that a paper label was ridiculous, it would never last. Mum had sent in an order for more of the ink and written out a little sign to put on the counter, offering free cloth squares with every bottle sold.

Molly decided she would probably have to rip the label out again, once she'd run away. It would be too dangerous to have her name and address there for anyone who happened to glance at her coat lining. She leaned up on her elbow and peered over at Stella. It was too dark to see her properly, even though her eyes were used to it a bit by now. Stella was still just a rounded hump under the blankets. But she definitely sounded asleep. Molly rolled silently out of the covers, and pulled the little case from under the bed. She'd packed it when she came up to bed, dragging it out of the back of the wardrobe and flinging in everything she could find while Stella was in the lavatory. Her other dress, the yellow cardigan Stella had knitted. Some socks and a couple of hankies. Her summer plimsolls – they were a bit small, but they might be useful. The case scuffed along the floor as she pulled it, and Stella gave a little snort and a twitch. Molly froze. But then her sister sighed and went back to sleep. Molly scooped up the dress she'd worn the day before from the chair in the corner of the room, and crept out. She'd put it on down in the kitchen.

Molly scurried down the stairs with the case and frantically shushed Bertie, who was leaping about, delighted to see her so early. It was hard not to fall over him in the dimness of the kitchen. She crouched down, rubbing his ears and murmuring, "Ssshhh! Good boy, ssshhh... Don't bark, don't bark."

Was it safe to turn on the light? Molly pulled down the switch and stood by it, frozen. With the doors shut upstairs, surely her mother and Stella wouldn't notice. She opened the little case on the table and pushed her nightdress in with the clothes she'd grabbed the night before.

Molly fetched her coat and started to do it

up – and then she remembered that Sally and Jean had been wearing labels tied around their buttons. Not fabric labels like the one Stella had sewn into her coat, but proper printed ones with the name of the school on too. If she wanted to slip into a group, or even just look as though she was supposed to be at the station, she needed one of those. *Do we sell luggage labels in the shop?* Molly thought, biting at her bottom lip. She'd never seen them, but then the shop was so full of packets of this and that, she just might not have noticed. She shut the little case, wondering if she could get away without, and then she laughed and pressed her hand over her mouth to muffle the noise.

There was already a label on the case. It was a little faded and worn, and it was written on one side – her father's name, Alfred Mason, and the address of the shop – but the other side was quite clean. Her father's leaking old fountain pen stood in a coronation mug on the dresser, and Molly picked it up reverently. Neither Mum nor Stella ever used it, but Molly felt that her father's pen was what she needed. She had taken it out of the mug a few times before when no one was around to see her, trying out the last remnants of ink on an old paper bag, or a bus ticket. The pen wrote beautifully, in thick, dark ink. It would make her label look official, or at any rate more official than a pencil, or Mum's scratchy dip pen.

Carefully, in her best looping cursive, Molly wrote her name and then her address. She couldn't quite remember what Jean's and Sally's labels had said, but they were printed, anyway, so hers wasn't going to pass if someone looked at it properly. It might do for a quick glance, though.

Next to the mug where the pen was kept was the old china mustard jar, where Mum kept the housekeeping money. Molly hadn't intended to take money with her, but once she'd seen it she couldn't look away. She reached it down and set it on the table, staring at it. She did *need* some money. She had to take it. She was expecting that there would still be trains full of evacuees going out of London, but if there weren't, she'd have to buy a ticket. It was only the money that Mum would have spent to feed her and Bertie, Molly reasoned to herself. But it still made her stomach twist to count out ten shillings. It felt like stealing, a lot more than borrowing the case did. There was still a bit left in the jar, she hadn't taken *all* of it, which made her feel a little better, but not much.

Would ten shillings even be enough? Molly had never bought a train ticket – she'd never been on a train, she'd never needed to. She didn't even know where she was going. Jean's mum hadn't said exactly where they were, just that it was near Hereford. Anyway, even if she did know, it was probably better not to try and follow them. Sally was terrible at keeping secrets; she'd be bound to write the news to her mum.

Molly would just have to get as far away as she could, and then start walking.

With the money tucked away safely in her coat

pocket, Molly was reaching for Bertie's lead on the hooks by the back door with the gas masks when she saw Tom. He was crouched on the top of the dresser, glaring down at her, obviously wondering what on earth was going on. He and Bertie knew the household routine, and it was clearly too early for anyone to be up.

Molly dropped her hand. She was all ready. She had her coat and shoes on, and even her winter beret, since she didn't know how long she was going to be away. She only had to clip on Bertie's lead, and they would be gone.

But what about Tom? It was Bertie she had been worrying about, ever since the boy had told her what was happening. Even though it had been Mum fussing over Tom that had first made her suspect, Molly hadn't ever meant to take him too.

She didn't even like him.

He wasn't a sweet, purry sort of cat – except sometimes for Mum. He knew which side his bread was buttered, Stella said. She called him a ginger devil, since it was always her shoes he decided to leave his mouse tails in.

Tom would let someone stroke him, and look as though he was perfectly happy, and then whip round and have a chunk out of their hand. But still... If Molly left him here, Mum and Stella were going to have him put to sleep. The wicker basket was sitting in the corner of the stockroom, behind a box of babies' hats, ready. As if they thought she wouldn't notice.

She might not like Tom, but that didn't mean she wanted that to happen to him. Sighing, she went to fetch the basket, flinching every time the wicker creaked. Tom was still on top of the dresser, though, and he didn't look as though he was planning to come down. "Puss, puss..." Molly whispered hopefully, but he only tucked his paws underneath him tighter and turned to stare sideways at the wall. It was such an obvious slight that Molly almost laughed.

Molly undid the wire door of the meat safe,

and unwrapped a greaseproof parcel of greasy leftover bacon, wafting it temptingly towards the suspicious cat. She was sure that Tom knew this was all a ploy – his tail tip was twitching – but Molly could smell the bacon, rich and salty, and so could Bertie. He was wriggling next to her, practically dribbling.

"Come on," Molly whispered pleadingly, and Tom stood up. He arched his back and yawned, as if he couldn't be less interested in what she was doing. Then he scrabbled down the side of the dresser and on to the edge of the sink, and waited for her to bring the bacon to him.

Molly fed him a scrap, shivering a little as his tongue rasped over her fingers, and then another piece, big enough that he had to chew. Then she dropped the packet and grabbed him round the middle, squashing him into the open basket.

For such a soft, furry thing, he was suddenly all legs and claws and angles, and he tore great bleeding scratches down both of her hands before she got the lid down, but Molly did get him in. She shoved the little catch on the basket across, and sucked her scratches. She couldn't wash them, the pipes would rattle.

Bertie looked up at her happily, licking the last of the bacon from round his muzzle. He'd eaten the paper as well, Molly realized, a little worriedly. She hoped it wouldn't do anything awful to his insides. Still, at least he'd had breakfast. Molly clipped his lead on and picked up the hissing basket. They'd better go quickly, before Tom lost his temper entirely and started to yowl. She still wasn't sure it was a good idea to take him, but she just couldn't bring herself to leave him behind.

"You might at least be a bit grateful," she muttered as the basket shook violently, and she almost dropped it. "Keep still!" She unlocked the back door, and padded quietly across the yard. Then she had to set everything down again to unlatch the yard gate that led out into the back alley. Tom's basket didn't have a handle, so she had to tuck it under one arm, and hold the case and Bertie's lead with the other. Her arms were aching before she'd even got out on to the street, and Tom was hissing like a kettle. It didn't help that Bertie was fascinated by the noise he was making, and kept trying to jump up and sniff the basket. Molly struggled along the road muttering "Ssshhh!" and "Stop it!" and trying not to bump into lamp posts. It was frighteningly dark. She hadn't been out in the blackout until now, and she hadn't realized how difficult it would be – how much difference the lamplight really made. She couldn't see anything more than a foot or so in front of her. She was thankful that Bertie was mostly white – if he'd been a black dog she would have kept falling over him.

Molly had been quite sure that she knew the way to Liverpool Street, the main line station that her school had been heading for, but the darkness seemed to have turned all the streets around, and after half an hour of stumbling, inching steps, she realized it was no good. She couldn't be more than two streets away from home, surely, but she was lost. Completely and utterly. She stopped, trying to tuck the basket up under her arm again. It felt so heavy, and Tom kept wriggling, which made it even harder to hold on to.

At that moment, Bertie lost patience with this slow walking and tried to leap up at Tom again. Molly was still struggling to balance the basket under her arm, and when Bertie jumped up she lost her grip completely. The basket crashed to the pavement, and the flimsy catch fell apart. Tom burst out, spitting, and hared away down the street, a faint creamy-ginger blur in the darkness.

Molly gazed down at Bertie reproachfully and he whined, ducking his head. He looked a little guilty, but not very. Tom was gone – there was no sign of him at all.

"I suppose he's run home. . ." Molly murmured, turning slowly in the darkness. Was it her imagination, or was the street a little lighter now?

Grey, rather than so heavily black. Dawn must be coming. If she went after Tom now, she'd probably end up finding Mum in the kitchen boiling the kettle. But if she left him behind...

Molly sighed and picked up the broken basket and the case, taking a firmer grip on Tom's lead. "It's all very well for him, cats can see in the dark..." she whispered to herself. She walked on, feeling for each step in case there was a pillar box, or someone's rubbish left out, or a sign. She'd never realized before how many things there were to bump into. Some of the road signs had a little luminous paint dabbed on them to help, but most of them didn't.

On she went, still hoping to see Tom scowling back at her around the next corner – except they didn't know which way he'd gone – and then the pavement just wasn't there any more, and she stumbled, half-falling down a kerb. "Oh, he *is* a ginger devil!" she hissed to Bertie, rubbing at her twisted ankle. "It's no use at all! The basket's broken and, anyway, I'd never catch him. He probably won't let me near him for weeks now, not after I stuffed him in this stupid thing." She swallowed, remembering that Tom didn't have weeks. Although, if Mum and Stella hadn't got a basket to put him in, perhaps they wouldn't take him to the vet after all? She could hope, at least.

Molly set the battered basket down in a shop doorway, and sat on it. "Did you break it open on purpose?" she asked Bertie, who slumped down next to her with a sigh, nose on paws. Molly reached down to stroke him. "Maybe you didn't want him along? I didn't much want him either, but I don't want them to – to—" She wasn't actually sure how the vet would destroy a cat. She'd heard of kittens being drowned, but surely a vet wouldn't do that?

The stockroom back at the shop was full of boxes, all cat-sized.

"But I expect he's so furious he won't even let Mum near him," Molly suggested to Bertie hopefully. "They wouldn't be able to catch him, even if they did find something else to put him in."

Molly looked around. She had no idea where she was now – it was still too dark to see what the shop was selling, even. They were going to have to wait until it was lighter to set out again. She could only hope that she hadn't turned herself around so much that she was sitting on her own front doorstep.

Chapter Five

Sometime later, Molly jerked awake from a dream of chasing Tom through endless grey streets. She jumped up, her heart thudding in her throat. It was getting properly light now, and she could see someone undoing the metal shutters on one of the shops further down the road. "Bertie, come on. We went to sleep. I didn't mean to – I just sat down for a bit. Oh, we're late, come on." She snatched up the case and looked doubtfully at the basket. She didn't want to carry it with her, but she felt bad abandoning it on the step of the shop. Perhaps they'd be able to make use of it, she decided, glancing anxiously at the golden sky. Now that it was light, she could see that she wasn't far from home at all. In fact, she was at the end of the road where the vet was, she realized, looking around in disgust. She had gone in the right direction at least, but she'd hoped to be at Liverpool Street by the time it was light. She didn't actually know when the trains started running, Molly admitted to herself as she and Bertie hurried on. Perhaps it was better to be a bit late? Wouldn't it look suspicious if she was too early? If she was hoping to sneak herself into a party of children being evacuated, she needed the station to be busy.

As she came close enough to see the brick towers of the station over the shops, Molly saw the first group of children, walking along the other side of the road. They looked so like the children from her own school – the little ones huddling together or clinging on to their sisters and brothers – that Molly almost ran towards them, hoping to see Sally or Jean. She searched along the line of children, all bundled up in winter clothes because no one knew when they'd be back, all lugging cases and bundles. Then she flushed pink as a strange girl stared back at her. Sally and Jean had gone three days before, of course. She was being stupid.

Molly looked down at her feet, avoiding the girl's curious glance. She mustn't do that. She mustn't let anyone notice her, or remember her. She had to slide in amongst everyone else. Like a spy. The line of children passed her, and Molly followed a little way behind. She had never been into the station, and she didn't know which way she was supposed to go in. The building was vast, with turrets and towers and signs everywhere, and taxis gliding down a sloping entranceway and right inside the station itself.

The neat crocodile of children vanished along a walkway beside the taxis and under an arch, and Molly scurried after them.

The narrow entrance past the shops was dim

after the bright morning, and Molly blinked as she came out into the main hall of the station. She had expected it would be so full of children and fussing school staff that she could just tag on to a large group. The teachers couldn't know every single child, after all. It should be easy enough. One of the women who came into the shop on Friday had followed her children all the way to the station to say goodbye. She had told Stella that the place was heaving with children being packed on to trains in great chattering crowds. There was even a man from the BBC, she'd said, interviewing the children and getting them to cheer as they climbed aboard the trains. But no one would let her go on to the platform, and she had to stand at the metal gate and watch her little girl walk to a train by herself, staring back at her all the way. Then the woman started to cry, leaning on the counter, and Stella had sent Molly to fetch a drink of water for her.

Molly ducked back against the wall of a

newspaper stand out of the way and looked around, clutching tightly on to Bertie's lead.

The station wasn't packed with children, as she'd thought it would be. Perhaps she was too late, Molly thought worriedly. She should have tried this on Friday, but she hadn't known then. . . On Friday she had been feeling sorry for herself, left behind when all the others went off on their exciting adventure. Looking back, it seemed almost silly. She had been so angry with her mother, and that had been nothing. Nothing compared to doing away with Bertie – and Tom. Molly grimaced and tried not to think of Tom.

Bertie whined a little, and Molly felt his stubby tail flick against her leg. He was fascinated, she realized as she shushed him. The station might not be as full as she had hoped, but there were still people hurrying everywhere. A train must have just come in, as men in dark suits and bowler hats were starting to pour past her now, marching out into the city for the start of their working day. There were a few women too, here and there among the suits. None of them paid the least bit of attention to the worried-looking child lurking in the shadows by the newspapers, or the excited dog quivering at her feet.

The line of schoolchildren had gathered at the entrance to one of the platforms, and Molly wondered if she should follow them. She couldn't see well enough back here, she realized as she was trying to work out if there were more groups waiting on other platforms. The station was so confusing, cut in half by the roadway, and spiderwebbed with iron walkways carrying passengers overhead. She would have to go further in.

"Come on," she murmured to Bertie, and then, "*Please* be good." He was, usually, but he'd never been anywhere so busy and fascinating before. He was either excited or terrified, and she couldn't tell which. And she wasn't at all sure how he was going to feel about trains. She wasn't sure how she felt about them either. She'd been on the Underground once, with Stella, but that was different. The Underground trains felt to Molly as if they were contained within the tunnels – they were held, and safe. The steam trains she had seen at the cinema looked wild and almost angry.

This time she tucked herself against one of the great metal columns that held up the glass roof. From here she could see more of the station, but she could be seen too.

She felt safer with something solid at her back – as though no one could creep up on her. And it meant there was still a heavy lump of metal between her and those great dark trains. There was one drawing in now on a further platform, so heavy and powerful that Molly could feel the ground under her feet shaking, the air shaking. Its whistle shrieked and Bertie set off a furious yapping.

"Look, *she* has her dog!" a small voice complained, and Molly flinched back against the column.

"Ssshhh, Vicky!" Molly risked a glance, and saw

a small girl staring at her accusingly. She looked a little younger than Molly, and she was with a group of girls in a grey school uniform, snaking across the station in pairs. The girl's bigger sister was trying to pull her along, so they weren't left behind amongst all the hurrying travellers, but she was leaning back to look at Bertie, dragging against her sister so fiercely that she was almost horizontal.

"Chips will be fine," the older one assured her. "He's got to stay behind and keep Mummy company, Vicky. She'd be lonely otherwise."

"She's got Daddy," the little girl said stubbornly. "I wanted to take Chips, he's *my* dog, I got him for *my* birthday."

"Well, school said no dogs. Come on, Vicky, we're getting left behind!' And the older one jerked her hand sharply, so that she stumbled after her with a wail.

Molly sucked in a breath. She certainly couldn't sneak in amongst that lot, with their smart school uniform and posh accents. But it was clear that

Bertie was going to be a problem, even if she could find a school group more like her own. No one else was being evacuated with a dog. Molly looked at her case, and sighed. He wouldn't fit, and even if he did she'd never make him stay quiet, he'd probably be worse than Tom.

That girl, though… She'd been wearing a blazer, but she'd had an overcoat too, slung over her shoulder, since she was trying to manage a suitcase and a little sister. It was a warm day already, quite warm enough not to be wearing a coat. Molly had her cardigan on underneath, and she was stifling. Molly shrugged the coat off and crouched down, draping it over Bertie. He peered up at her indignantly and shimmied backwards, trying to get out from underneath, but Molly pulled the coat around him tight.

"Ssshhh…" she whispered. "Just a cuddle, Bertie. Ssshhh." She scooped him up in her arms, pretending that he was a fat bundle of winter coat – one that was letting out a thin, unhappy growl. She couldn't wait any longer, she decided. Bertie wasn't going to put up with this for any amount of time, and the clock hanging high above her said that it was past eight already. Mum and Stella were probably out looking for her by now. She must try to get herself on to a train.

She stumbled along the station, with her bundle of dog tucked up under her chin and her case banging against her legs. She wasn't going to be able to manage Bertie and the case for long.

"Did you get lost, dear?"

Molly jumped, and nearly lost her grip on Bertie. She turned slowly to find a man in a uniform peering down at her from under a peaked cap. A ticket inspector, she guessed. She swallowed hard. "Yes. . . I stopped to take my coat off, and then – and then they were gone!" It was all too easy to sound as though she was about to cry.

"Poor little love. Don't worry, we'll find them. Which group are you with? Where's your label? On your coat, is it?" He reached out to take the coat from her, and Molly jerked it away. If he looked properly at the label, he'd know she wasn't with a party, not to mention that Bertie would probably bite him.

"I'm not going to take it off you, lovey, I just want a look, that's all. Then I can help you find the rest of your school." The man sounded slightly exasperated, and he was reaching out for the coat again. Molly shook her head and forced a smile. "I can see them! They're by that train. Thanks, mister!" She snatched up her case and stumbled away, trying to ignore the growls from her coat. She didn't look back – she wanted to, but if she did, he'd know she was lying, she was sure. Instead she darted around a tall signboard and whispered soothingly to Bertie. "Just a little longer, that's all. Good dog."

Her coat wagged, and the growling subsided a little, but she could feel the tension in him, the way he was ready to spring out and dash away as soon as he had the chance. She tried to hold him more gently – Bertie liked to sit in her lap or Stella's, after all – but she needed one hand for the case, so she couldn't help huddling Bertie and the coat up in her other arm. Molly peered round the edge of the signboard, wondering if the station worker had believed her. He was still standing by the pillar, looking official. If he saw her again, on her own, he'd know that she'd lied to him.

Molly set her shoulders back and sighed. The children she had wildly pointed out were the smartly dressed ones, the group that the little girl who'd wanted to bring her dog belonged to. There were quite a lot of them, she saw now, bulging out of their neat crocodile as they gathered around a platform gate. They had on neat grey tunics under their grey coats. Molly's dress was blue, but at least her coat was the right colour – only it was wrapped around a dog. Molly set down the bundle of coat and Bertie, keeping her foot on the end of his lead in case he realized what was happening and tried to make a run for it, and swiftly unbuttoned her cardigan. Then she whisked Bertie out of her coat and swathed the cardigan around him instead. He glared up at her indignantly, and Molly sighed. "I know," she whispered, trying to shrug her coat on and keep hold of him at the same time. "But it's all lacy, isn't it? You can see through the holes now."

There was a toffee in her pocket, Molly remembered. She hadn't eaten it because it had gone all sticky and she couldn't get the paper off, but Bertie wouldn't mind. She held it just above his nose, and he snatched it out of her hand as if he were starving. The cardigan didn't disguise him quite as well as the coat had, but it would do.

Slowly, she began to drift across the station, trying to move from one group of people to another, so that she looked as though she belonged. The school party all had the same hats, she realized as she came closer, felt hats with some sort of school badge. Perhaps she could pretend she'd lost hers, or left it behind. She pulled off her knitted beret and stuffed it into her coat pocket. They were starting to move through the metal gates now, on to the platform, and Molly scurried faster, darting in behind the pair of sisters. They were still arguing.

"I carried it all the way from the bus," the smaller one hissed. "And you're bigger, you have to carry it now, Sarah, it's not fair!"

Her older sister stalked ahead with her nose in the air, and called back, "Hurry up, Vicky! And do stop whining!"

Molly ducked her head a little as she went past the ticket collector at the gate, but it was just as she'd hoped, the school party were going through without tickets, or perhaps their teachers had them all. At any rate, he didn't stop her. She simply followed on, marching down the platform with the others.

"In here, then," called a woman in a sensible sort of hat. "Yes, you two, and you, there's plenty of room. Yes, eight of you, perfect. Goodness, what *is* that bundle? Really, girls, I do think you could have packed better, you all look terribly untidy."

Molly slunk across the train corridor and into the compartment. At least the woman hadn't noticed that she didn't have a hat. She settled on the edge of the high-backed seat, and clutched tightly at her cardigan, in case the teacher tried to put it up on top of the luggage rack with the cases.

The older of the two sisters started to complain but her teacher was having none of it. "Don't argue, Sarah, it's absolutely irrelevant that you promised Gwen, Gwen is at least two compartments away and I don't have time to bother with you now. In here, please."

"Beast," Sarah muttered as the teacher hurried them all in, and then whirled round to chase down a small grey-clad girl dashing along the corridor.

"Elspeth! Back here at once! No running!"

"I promised Gwen I'd sit with her," Sarah growled, slumping back on to the seat so hard that a little puff of dust came up. "I *promised* her, and now she'll be sitting with Meg, while I'm stuck with a bunch of little Firsts. And Meg hates me! By the time we get off this nasty, dirty train neither of them will be talking to me ever again."

"Now you have to sit with me," her younger sister said smugly. "I told you Miss Reynolds said sisters were staying together. You should have listened."

"Shut up!" Sarah snapped, kicking the wooden frame of the seat. She glared around at the other children in the compartment – five more girls around her sister's age, and Molly – as if she was daring to them to so much as smirk. Then she leaned forward, staring at Molly and wrinkling her nose.

"Who are you? You're not in Vicky's class, and you're certainly not in the Upper Third." She rolled her eyes. "Typical. Miss Reynolds sticks us with some useless little new bug."

"You're probably supposed to look after her, Sarah," one of the others put in shyly. "She looks like she might be the same age as you."

Sarah heaved a sigh. "So how old are you?" she demanded, scowling at Molly.

Molly swallowed hard. Surely they'd know she wasn't one of them as soon as she opened her mouth. But they were horrible enough that she could pretend to be shy, maybe. "Nine," she whispered.

"Then you'll be in the Second, not with me! I'm going to find Miss Reynolds and tell her." Sarah bounced up, and peered out round the compartment's sliding door. "She's gone haring off after Elspeth. I suppose I could just *take* you to the Seconds. . ."

"Oh, no!" all the others twittered.

"You can't, Sarah."

"You'll get into trouble!"

Molly only just stopped herself from rolling her eyes. Did it really matter that much where she sat? Then again, she'd probably have made a fuss if she'd been allowed to go with school and she'd been separated from Sally and Jean.

"Sarah, do you think we're allowed to take our hats off?" a small fair girl asked. "She hasn't got hers on."

Molly felt her shoulders hunch over as all seven girls eyed her even more severely.

"The rules say hats on whenever St Anne's girls are out in public," Sarah muttered. "But this isn't public exactly, is it? If we're in a train?"

"Did your mother not get all your things?" the fair girl asked Molly now. "Because I'm sorry to say, your uniform isn't right at all. It's awful, actually. You've got brown shoes on, and white socks. St Anne's girls have to be properly dressed at all times. You'll get endless order marks, you know. You'll be letting down everyone in your form."

"It might be different now we're evacuated," Vicky put in. "And they wouldn't give order marks to a new girl, Lottie, don't be mean. Not even Miss Hilton would do that."

"She would! She gave me an order mark because I had one sock pulled up higher than the other, so imagine what she'd say about *white* socks!" Lottie folded her arms impressively. "Anyway, I'm going to take my hat off." She did, but she sat holding it on her lap, looking worried. She clearly expected Miss Reynolds or the dreaded Miss Hilton to leap out from under the seats, Molly thought, trying not to grin.

"Oh, we're going!" Vicky stood up and ran to the door, and Molly caught the edge of the seat, digging her nails into the bristly velveteen. Vicky was right. She could feel the train lurching beneath her, and the faint veils of smoke and steam that had been drifting past the windows suddenly thickened. Vicky caught her arm, pulling her along. "Come and see! Let's wave!"

Molly hastily grabbed Bertie again, and let the littler girl pull her out into the corridor. The glass in the train door was pushed down, and Vicky leaned out of it, ignoring her sister's hissed instructions to come back this instant.

"I love it when trains start, don't you?" Vicky

was hanging out of the window, looking down the platform. "I wish we could see the engine."

There was a strange coughing noise as the engine began to move away, and Molly closed her eyes, trying not to see the platform sliding backwards. It made her feel dizzy. The coughing settled into a more rhythmic growl as the train started to gather speed, and Molly could feel Vicky hopping excitedly beside her, until Sarah gave up trying to persuade them back in, and decided just to drag them instead.

"You'll be covered in smuts, come back here!" she snapped. "And you, whatever your name is, come on!"

Molly opened her eyes to find the two sisters squabbling next to her – and Bertie objecting to the squeals, and the smoke, and the juddering of the train.

"What – is – that?" Sarah gasped as he wriggled out of Molly's cardigan at last, and barked furiously at her.

"Oh, it's *you*!" Vicky cried. "We saw you before!"

Sarah seized Molly's wrist and pulled her back into the compartment and on to the seat, with Vicky next to her. "Miss Hilton *never* allowed you to bring your dog. I don't believe it," she said flatly, stooping over her and staring.

Bertie snarled, and Molly grabbed him with both hands. He'd never bitten her, but she wouldn't put it past him to nip at Sarah, the way she was leaning so close.

Sarah jumped back, looking angry. "And he's vicious!"

"He isn't! He just doesn't like you!"

Vicky started to laugh, and Sarah flushed scarlet, and looked crosser than ever. "I don't believe you're even part of our school," she said slowly. "That's not a St Anne's coat. You don't have a school badge on it. You little liar!"

"I never lied," Molly said, still trying to hold Bertie back. "I never said anything. You were the one who went on and on about your precious Upper Third."

"What are you doing on our train?" Lottie asked, staring.

Molly eyed her coldly. "Your train? It doesn't belong to you."

"We have tickets for it, and these compartments were reserved for St Anne's," Sarah spat back. "It is our train."

"Are you with the wrong school?" The girl on the other side of Vicky looked at Molly worriedly. "Did you get mixed up at the station? There was another school, I saw them, but I thought they had a navy uniform. Maybe we should go and find Miss Reynolds."

"No. It'll end up being our fault." Sarah scowled. "I don't believe you're with a school at all. That isn't a school uniform." She pulled at Molly's coat, showing the blue cotton dress underneath.

"Get off me!" Molly snapped, shoving her hand away, and Bertie growled again, the deep rumbling growl that always sounded as if it belonged to a bigger dog.

Sarah darted back, but she only looked daunted for a moment. "I'm right though, aren't I?" She glanced round at the other girls triumphantly. "Look at her! She doesn't belong to anyone!"

Molly opened her mouth to answer back – of course she belonged to someone! She had Mum and Stella, and everyone at Hanley Road. But then she found she couldn't say anything. It was true. Since she'd found out what Mum was planning, all she'd done was race ahead, knowing that she had to stop Bertie being destroyed. She had planned and fought, and not ever stopped to think that she was tearing herself out of a family.

She didn't belong now, and she couldn't go back.

Chapter Six

"You made her cry!" Vicky told her sister accusingly, but Sarah didn't look as though she cared. She sat back on the train seat and folded her arms.

"I wonder what we should do with you."

"You're not doing anything with me. Just mind your own business." Molly glared back at her, and then blinked hard. She did feel like crying, but she wasn't yet, not quite. And she certainly wasn't going to in front of *them*

"But you are our business." Vicky edged closer to Molly, and offered Bertie the back of her hand to sniff. "You're here in our compartment. And you can't say you're meant to be, because we know that you're not really a new girl. So what are you doing?"

"Don't have to tell you anything," Molly muttered. She was still trying to work out what to do. Sarah's mean little comment and jeering look had turned everything upside down. Her plan had been all about getting away, and not what she was going to do once she'd managed it. Back at home, when her choice had been to run, or to accept that Bertie would be killed, the answer had been obvious. Now – she was still sure she had done the right thing, but perhaps she wasn't doing it very well...

It wasn't as if she'd had a lot of time to work all these things out, Molly told herself as she tried to avoid Vicky's sympathetic eyes. She didn't want people worrying about her, it was making everything feel a lot worse.

"Are you running away from the bombs?" the fair one, Lottie, asked, so earnestly that her pale blue eyes bulged.

"Ssshh." The girl next to her elbowed her in the side. "That's rude. Just because she doesn't go to a good school, it doesn't mean she's a wimp."

Molly frowned. Stuck-up little brats. "What do you think you're all doing then? You're running away."

"No, we aren't," Sarah snapped. "The school's being relocated. So our parents can concentrate on the war effort."

"That's the same as running away."

"Obviously we'd all rather stay and face the music." Sarah looked down her nose. "We just don't have a choice. Anyway, you're on your own and you look like you're running away to me, and I don't see why. Wasn't your school evacuated?"

Molly sighed. She was going to be on this train for hours, probably. She wasn't sure how far they needed to go to get to the reception area, where everything was supposed to be safe, but it was bound to be a good long way. If she wanted these girls on her side, she was going to have to tell them

113

something, and at least the truth was easy. She wouldn't have to make something up and then remember what she'd said to who. Besides, Vicky clearly liked dogs. Perhaps Bertie would get a bit of sympathy, and they wouldn't shop her to that Miss Reynolds.

"It was. But my mum said I couldn't go. She said she'd rather we all died together."

There was a sharp intake of breath around the train compartment, and Molly realized she'd made a mistake. Of course, all these girls had parents who were staying in London.

"I mean, if anything happened. But she was pretty sure it wasn't going to," Molly added quickly.

Sarah was scowling at her again. She was older, probably eleven or twelve. She had more of an idea of what was happening than the littler girls. And she was the one who would be stuck in a train compartment with them if Molly sent them all hysterical. Molly hurried on, trying to cover up. "But then I heard my mum and my sister talking last night. . ." Had it only been last night? It seemed a lot longer ago.

"What did they say?" Lottie asked breathlessly at last, and Molly looked around each of them – she hadn't meant to leave a dramatic pause, but it had worked.

"My mum said that when the bombs started falling, dogs were going to be so frightened they'd be dangerous. She said Bertie might go wild and it would be cruel to keep him in London."

"I'm not surprised," Sarah muttered, but she looked just as interested as the smaller girls.

"Sssshhh!" Vicky grimaced at her. "Go on. What happened? What else did your mother say?"

"She told my sister that she had to take Bertie to the vet to be put to sleep. Because otherwise he'd suffer when the bombing started." Molly felt Bertie wriggle protestingly, and realized that she'd been hugging him far too tight.

"Put to sleep?" the smallest of the girls asked, frowning. She was sitting on Molly's other side, a tiny, curly-haired child who Molly reckoned couldn't be more than seven. "What do you mean, put to sleep?"

"It doesn't matter, Daphne," Sarah said quickly. "Don't listen to her, she's lying."

"No, I'm not!" Molly protested, but then she saw Sarah watching her little sister. Vicky's face had drained of all colour, so that she looked a sickly yellow.

"Sarah. . ."

"That isn't what's going to happen to Chips," Sarah said sharply.

Molly ducked her head, and rubbed her cheek against Bertie's soft ears. She hadn't meant to upset them again. She didn't seem to be able to say anything right with this lot. She'd only wanted them to feel sorry for her and Bertie.

"Mummy wouldn't, would she?" Vicky whispered. "She promised she'd look after him. She absolutely promised."

"My mum said people who could afford it were

supposed to send their dogs to the country. Like the kids," she told Vicky. "Maybe that's what your mum will do. If you've got relatives in the country?"

"Exactly." Sarah nodded eagerly. "Mummy could send Chips to Auntie Lydia. Don't get into a state, Vicky."

Vicky lifted her head. "When we get there, to this house in Suffolk that's going to be our new school, I'm writing to Mummy first thing! I don't care what Miss Reynolds says, or even Hitler! I'm doing it as soon as we get there and then I'm going to find a postbox. I'm going to make Mummy promise that she isn't having him put to sleep!"

"I still don't know what that means!" Daphne wailed. "Why shouldn't Chips go to sleep? Is it to do with the war? What's wrong with sleeping?"

"Sleeping's just a nice way of saying that someone's died," Molly told her. "It means the vet doing something to – to kill them." Then she added quickly, "Sorry," as everyone looked at her disapprovingly. Obviously it just wasn't good manners to talk about such things, but Molly didn't see the point in hiding it. It *was* what they were doing, after all.

"Oh. . ." Daphne sat back, looking shocked. "But . . . but Chips is a good dog. He can shake a paw, and roll over, I've seen him do it when I came to tea. And your dog isn't fierce. He hasn't snapped. He growled a little bit when Sarah grabbed you, that was all."

"Mum thought the bombs would send him funny, though."

"That's not fair!" Daphne sounded so indignant, Molly almost laughed.

"I know. That's why we ran away. My mum. . . I mean, once she's decided something. . . You can't make her change her mind. You just can't. My sister went to join the ATS and my mum said if she did she'd have to leave home."

"Did she?" Sarah asked interestedly.

Molly shook her head. "It's the only time my sister's ever won. Stella said she didn't care, and my mum gave in. But it's the *only* time, I mean it. She wasn't going to give in about Bertie, I knew she wasn't. She doesn't even like him. So I had to take him and go."

Vicky got up and went to stand in front of Sarah, holding on to the side of the seat. "If we tell Miss Reynolds she's here, Miss Reynolds will send her back." She turned back to Molly. "What's your name? You told us your dog's name, but not yours."

Molly only hesitated for a second or two. "Molly Mason."

"Miss Reynolds will send Molly back, and Bertie. She might even call the police, Sarah!"

"She isn't anything to do with us," Sarah muttered, but she looked uncomfortable about it.

"It's wrong!" Vicky hissed. "It's like Daphne said, he's a good dog! Look at him!"

Bertie gazed back at them all, ears pricked. He was relaxed now, sitting comfortably on Molly's lap, and panting a little. Daphne was stroking him, and he looked quite smug.

"He hasn't done anything," Vicky went on. "How can it be right to have him put to sleep? That's what will happen, if we don't help her. Sarah, please. Please don't tell on her."

"You said she isn't anything to do with us," Lottie said. "So couldn't you just pretend you don't know anything about her? We all thought she must be a new girl, didn't we? We could just go on thinking that." She folded her hands in her lap and looked saintly. She reminded Molly of that box of chocs that Pearl had shared – it had a little fair girl with a kitten on the lid.

"Her uniform's all wrong!" Sarah protested.

"Only if you look close," Daphne said, eyeing Molly thoughtfully. "And it's wartime now. Mummy said school might not have to fuss about uniform so much because it'll be hard to get the right clothes."

"I don't think that counts when we've only been at war since yesterday," Vicky said, but she said it kindly.

"Miss Reynolds is still going to notice when she comes round to check on us," Sarah argued. "Which she'll probably do any minute." She heaved a sigh and glared at Molly. "You'd better go and sit in the corner. Be ready to put something over that horrible little dog. No, not your scruffy old cardigan," she added nastily, as Molly hastily swapped seats with one of the others. "Use Vicky's coat. Keep your coat on, and you can wear my gloves. If we all take our hats off, Miss Reynolds won't notice you don't have one."

"Oh, yes, good idea." Vicky took off her hat and climbed up on the seat to put it in the luggage rack. "Molly, shall I put your cardigan in your case? It's the wrong colour, you know. Miss Reynolds might see."

After all their preparations, Miss Reynolds merely glanced into the compartment as she hurried past a few minutes later, but Sarah seemed quite sure that she would be back.

"Where are you actually going?" she added,

as Bertie struggled grumpily out from under Vicky's coat.

Molly hesitated.

"Don't you *know*?" Vicky asked, almost admiringly.

"No one at my school knew where they were going last Friday." Molly shrugged, but she wasn't sure how convincing it was. "They just got marched off to get on a train. Do you know where you're going?"

"Oh yes. It's a house." Vicky looked over at Sarah. "I think it belongs to a friend of our headmistress. The school's moving into it. Mummy said—" And then she went pink and stopped.

Molly watched them all looking embarrassed, and realized that Vicky and Sarah's mother had probably said that whoever owned the house would rather have a nice girls' school than a bunch of dirty little evacuee children, like her. She decided not to say anything.

"Where's this train going?"

"Suffolk. Well, I think this one's actually going to Norwich, and then we change."

"If she comes all the way to school with us, couldn't we say she's a new girl?" Daphne asked hopefully. "Then we could keep the dog." She scratched Bertie under the chin, and he pointed his nose to the ceiling in a state of pure bliss.

"Don't be silly, Daphne." Vicky shook her head. "As soon as anybody looks at her properly they'll know she isn't. And besides, they have lists. Lists and lists of all of us."

"We could hide her. . . I bet there's lots of hiding places in this house we're going to, and the staff haven't been there before. They'd never find her."

"Or there might be a secret underground passage she could live in," Vicky agreed thoughtfully.

"Don't be idiotic." Sarah sighed. "You read too many adventure stories. It's just going to be a boring old house." She looked thoughtfully at Molly. "Will your mother report you missing?"

Molly felt her stomach turn over. She hadn't

even thought of that. There might be police chasing after her and Bertie right now. "I suppose so," she said slowly. She wasn't sure whether to hope Mum would, or not. She didn't want anybody after them, of course. But wouldn't it be worse if no one cared enough to wonder where she'd gone? "She would," Molly added, more definitely.

"If anyone saw you at the station, they might be able to work out which train you got on."

Molly swallowed, fighting against the sudden lump of fear in her throat. "There was a guard – or somebody. In a railway uniform. He wanted to see my label, he thought I was lost. I told him I belonged with you."

"Oh well." Sarah shrugged. "That's torn it then, hasn't it?"

"What do you mean?" Vicky bounced on the seat. "What's wrong?"

"They'll find her, of course. If the police ask at the station, he's going to say that he saw Molly, and she got on the train with us."

"Maybe no one will bother, just now. Not with everything ... the way it is." Daphne looked hopefully between Molly and Sarah, and Molly tried not to mind that it was Bertie the little girl wanted to keep.

Sarah shook her head. "The police are still going to search for missing children."

She was right. Molly was pretty sure that Sarah was exaggerating because she wanted to get rid of her and Bertie, but that didn't mean she was wrong. She couldn't risk going on with the girls from St Anne's. "Is it big, Norwich Station?" she asked Sarah.

"I expect so. It's the county town, so it must be quite big. Big enough to disappear in, anyway."

"She's going?" Daphne asked sadly. "We can't keep them?"

"She isn't a pet, Daphne!"

There was a silence after that, broken only by Lottie passing round a bag of mint humbugs, and everyone sucking slowly. Molly leaned against the window, with Bertie curled in her lap, and watched the world slide by. This was a brief quiet moment, before they had to run again. She didn't want to go, she realized. Even though she didn't like Sarah, and the girls were more interested in Bertie than they were in her, the dusty, musty-smelling train compartment felt safe.

They were well out of London now, and the scene was mostly fields. It seemed odd to see so much open space, flat and green and topped by sky. She was used to walls. Even the park wasn't like this – emptiness all the way to the horizon, with just the odd small building here and there.

The train was surprisingly comfortable, she decided, once one got used to the rocking feeling. So rhythmic, juddering gently over the rails. Every so often they went through a station, but it seemed that the train wasn't due to stop at them all. It flew through them, just a few pale blurred faces watching on the platforms. When it did stop, no one got on or off. Molly yawned into her sleeve and tucked her chin down on her shoulder.

"Here, you mustn't fall asleep!"

Molly blinked awake to find Sarah shaking her. Lottie was asleep against her shoulder, and Daphne had her head pillowed on her folded coat. Sarah looked heavy-eyed too, as though maybe she'd just woken up.

"Someone has to stay awake to cover the dog up if any of the staff go by."

Molly nodded. "Sorry I won't fall asleep," she promised. But it was so hard not to, with the movement of the train, and the telegraph poles ticking past one after another...

"Good gracious!"

Molly jerked upright to find a tall woman staring down at her in horror. Miss Reynolds, she realized, pulling Vicky's coat over Bertie with slow, sleepy fingers. Far too late.

"There's no point trying to hide him," the teacher said sharply. "What on earth were you thinking?" Then she frowned, leaning down to look at Molly more closely. "Which form are you in?"

Molly blinked at her stupidly. She'd forgotten the plan. What was she supposed to say? Had they decided she could pretend to be a new girl, or was it no use?

"Honestly, child, who do you belong to? The Second? I thought I knew all of that form. . ." Miss Reynolds glanced round the compartment, and pounced on Sarah. The older girl had been right, Molly realized guiltily. She had said it would all end up being her fault. "Sarah, who is this child?"

Molly saw Sarah straighten her shoulders. She had been asleep too, Molly was fairly sure. Her hair was straggling sideways across her face, and her cheeks were flushed.

"Is she a new First Former?" Miss Reynolds asked impatiently.

Sarah shook her head. "No, Miss Reynolds. She – er – she isn't part of the school. She's being evacuated."

Miss Reynolds looked relieved for a moment – she didn't have to deal with a strictly forbidden dog – but then confused again. "But whatever is she doing on this train? All these compartments were reserved for the school. How did you end up here?" Her eyes widened gradually in a look of horror. "You're not meant to be with a different school? Did someone send you to us because of the grey uniform? Oh, goodness..."

Molly shook her head. "No, miss. I don't know why they said this train, miss." She shrugged, and tried to look both older and a little bit dim at the same time, but she had a feeling it wasn't working very well. The teacher seemed even more worried.

"Are you travelling alone?" she demanded, glancing around the compartment, as though she expected some sort of chaperone to leap out of the luggage rack.

"Yes, miss. But my aunt's meeting me at the other end."

"So where are you getting off the train?"

Molly blinked. Sarah had said – she'd told her the name of the station where they were changing, the big one where she'd be able to slip away. But it had gone out of her head entirely. She licked her lips nervously and slid her eyes sideways, hoping Sarah would mouth it to her. But Miss Reynolds was standing in between them.

"Isn't he a beautiful dog, Miss Reynolds?" Vicky said brightly. Molly thought she was trying to help, but it wasn't much good. She still couldn't think of the place.

"Yes," Miss Reynolds said impatiently. "Where are you going, child? Do you not know?" Her voice rose at the end of the sentence, in a way that suggested panic and police and everything going wrong.

"I'll recognize it when I see it," she said firmly.

"But you must have it written down," Miss Reynolds said, with a sudden relieved smile. "On your label? Or did your mother give you a piece of paper with your aunt's address?"

Molly looked down at her coat, her stomach turning over. Her address was on the label, she'd written it on herself. Now this busybody of a teacher was going to send her home. Except that the label wasn't there – only a chewed fragment of string, not even any of the paper left. Bertie had been bored while she was sleeping.

"I haven't got a label, miss," she said, shaking her head. "It's all right. My auntie's meeting me at the station."

"But *which one*?"

The train jolted a little, and Molly glanced sideways, out of the window. They were slowing down, drawing into a station. It was small, with brick buildings either side of the line, and a delicate latticed metal bridge between the two platforms.

"This one." She stood up. "Here, hold him a minute," she told Daphne, stuffing a confused Bertie into the little girl's arms. Then she clambered up on to the seat, surprising a horrified squeak from Miss Reynolds – but how else was she supposed to get her case down? As the train shuddered to a stop, Molly quickly pulled off her gloves and shoved them at Sarah. "Thanks," she said, not meaning it just for the loan. "Good luck then," she added.

Miss Reynolds peered out of the window at the station and turned back to Molly suspiciously. "How do you know? Which station is this?"

Molly tried to look out too, but she couldn't see a sign. "I know it's this one," she lied, not looking at her. "I recognize it, miss. Been to visit before, and I can see my auntie, she's waiting for me." Luckily she was between Miss Reynolds and the corridor now, and she hurried out, reaching for the door handle before the teacher could catch hold of her. She had a feeling Miss Reynolds didn't know whether to stop her or not – after all, Molly was nothing to do with her, not really. . .

"Oh!" Vicky started up from the seat, ripping the paper label from her coat button.

"Victoria, put that back," Miss Reynolds said sternly. "Those labels are absolutely essential." But Vicky was darting after Molly, trying to push the label into her hand. Molly was too busy with her suitcase, and Bertie, who had picked up on the excitement and was trying to eat his lead, so Vicky stuffed it into her coat pocket. Then she hugged Molly tightly, and whispered, "Write to us! Tell us what happens!" And she wrenched at the door handle, and shoved the train door open so Molly could hurry out. Looking back into the carriage, she could just see Daphne and Lottie and the others, even Sarah, all waving and jumping up and down, and somehow managing to be just in front of Miss Reynolds as she tried to follow. Molly elbowed the train door shut, and then jumped away as the train let out a wheezing shriek.

"Stand clear now!" bellowed an elderly man in a peaked cap, and Molly put down her case and waved wildly at the clutch of girls crowded around the window. Vicky was making scribbling gestures, and Daphne was calling goodbye to Bertie. A billow of choking steam flooded back up on to the platform from under the train's wheels, the engine coughed, and through the greyness Molly felt the heavy creature draw away.

When the steam thinned, she was alone on the platform, the train dwindling into the distance. Alone, and she had no idea where.

Chapter Seven

Even though the station looked deserted to Molly now, that man in the cap had to be around somewhere. He was probably the stationmaster, she reckoned. Would he want her ticket? Molly glanced cautiously up and down the platform, but he seemed to have disappeared. She had better go quickly, in case he came back.

"At least I don't have to carry you any more," she murmured to Bertie as they hurried around the side of the tiny ticket office and out on to a narrow road, lined by trees. Bertie didn't pay her the least bit of attention – he was too busy sniffing at the grass verge, clearly fascinated by all these new countryside smells.

It took Molly a little while to work out why the road felt so strange. It wasn't just the trees, and there not being any pavement, she realized after they had walked a couple of hundred yards. The road was empty. No one else was kicking up the dust at the side of the road like she was, and there were no cars or vans. She could hear an engine somewhere in the distance, but that was all. Empty, and eerily quiet. Why was the station in the middle of nowhere? Where were all the houses?

Molly walked on, tugging at Bertie's lead every so often. He wasn't worried about where they were going, or what happened now, she thought enviously as the little dog lunged after a passing butterfly and nearly pulled her over. It was hard to keep on walking when she didn't know what she was walking *to*. It did mean she couldn't be going the wrong way, which was a little bit comforting. Especially when they came to a place where two roads met, and signs pointed in opposite directions to different villages – Mclly had no idea which one she wanted. Still, if she followed one, and kept walking, she would come to – something.

She stood underneath the post, looking between the two boards. She wasn't even sure that walking into a village was a good idea. Miss Reynolds's horrified reaction to a child travelling on her own had left her feeling doubtful. When she ran away she'd vaguely thought that she would claim to be an evacuee. But it didn't look as though anyone was going to believe that, not if she turned up on her own. So far the war only seemed to mean gas masks and a lot of posters telling people to do things. There wasn't any of the confusion and panic that Molly had hoped would hide her and Bertie. Which was good, of course. It wasn't as if she wanted bombs to fall on people. But now what was she supposed to do?

It was becoming more and more obvious that Sarah had been right. Molly didn't belong anywhere. She would have to stay out of sight, she decided, with a last regretful look at the signs. For a while, at least.

By late afternoon – or it felt like late afternoon, anyway, and the sun was definitely going lower – Molly was regretting her choice. She had ripped out the label Stella had sewn in her coat, so surely no one could know who she was? They couldn't make her tell if she didn't want to. If she'd gone to the village there would have been food, along with all the questions.

A little way after the signpost, she had found a narrow track leading away from the road and through the fields. It had made sense to follow it, away from the villages. There was nothing along here but sheep. Now Molly was leaning on the fence watching them, with her hand woven tightly into Bertie's lead. He was far too interested in the sheep, and he kept growling at them and tugging at Molly. He didn't seem to care that he was a town dog, without the first idea how to herd sheep. He wanted to be in there, snapping at their heels.

"Stop it," Molly said wearily, pulling him back again. She should probably walk on and get him away from them, but she was trying to work out what sheep ate, and whether she and Bertie could eat it too. At least Bertie had gobbled down that piece of bacon that morning. She hadn't had anything since supper the night before, and she was so hungry it hurt. The sheep were eyeing Bertie – Molly thought they looked nervous about him. They were huddling together, and every so often one of them would stamp a foot. They were too worried to want to eat, Molly guessed, but there didn't seem to be any food bins around anyway, or even a manger.

Eventually, Bertie grew bored waiting, and slumped down in the long grass by Molly's feet. The sheep didn't seem as worried now they couldn't see him, and they started to wander away from their tight-knit group. Molly watched them hopefully. If she didn't let Bertie scare them again, surely they'd lead her to their food? But then two of the sheep put their heads down and began to graze slowly, tugging up the short, brownish late summer grass. Molly's heart sank, and she felt stupid. Sheep ate grass – she hadn't known that.

Could she eat it too? There were longer clumps by the gateposts, and the grass was a good colour, rich green and almost juicy-looking. She twisted a few of the tall stems around her fingers and pulled them up. It didn't really look like food, but she was desperate enough to try, nibbling at the thin tips.

It was horrible. Dry and crunchy and slimy all at the same time, and she spat it out, wiping her hand across her face in disgust. Bertie peered up at her in surprise, and Molly felt her eyes burning. She had managed not to cry on the train, but now she couldn't help it. The strange sweet taste of the grass was stuck in her mouth. She never ought to have come. It had been stupid to think she could run away, she was just stupid. Molly slumped down in the grass and rested her face on her knees, her shoulders heaving miserably.

Bertie snuffled at her, delighted that she was down on the ground with him and expecting her to play. But then he seemed to realize that she wasn't in a mood to roll around, and licked the line of her chin instead, and buried his chill nose in her ear.

"What are we going to do?" Molly gasped at him, between shudders. Eventually he climbed half into her lap, and tucked himself up under her chin. The solid lump of his skull pressed against her comfortingly, and Molly slowly caught her breath.

"Even if I could make myself eat grass, you definitely can't," she muttered at last. "All you want to do is chase those stupid sheep. I think people in the country shoot dogs if they do that."

Miss had read them something about that at school, she thought. About a dog being accused of chasing sheep. She wrapped her arms tighter round Bertie. He was still safer out here than he was in London with Mum.

The children whose dog had got into trouble had been out picking blackberries, Molly remembered now, brushing away tears with the sleeve of her cardigan. She might not know that sheep ate grass, but she did know what blackberries looked like. There were a few brambles growing along the alley that led from the yard behind the shop out to the street. There were never many blackberries on them, but she'd eaten one or two. They were a lot nicer than grass. Molly picked up her case and her coat, and set off further down the lane. It looked the sort of place that would have blackberry bushes.

She had been expecting the sort of spindly brambles she'd seen back at home, but when at last she found the blackberries, they were a great thicket, spilling over an old fence and sending out questing branches on to the path. The branches were heavy with fruit, black and red and green all at the same time, with even a few pinkish-white flowers here and there. They hardly seemed the same plant, and she stared at them doubtfully for a moment before she began cramming berries into her mouth. They were so sweet, some of them almost too sweet and overripe, but she didn't care, and she didn't care that her fingers were soon stained dark blood-red with juice, and pinprick scratches.

After a few minutes, Molly swallowed a mouthful of berries, and sighed. She wasn't full, but she felt a lot better, and she was worried about Bertie. He was used to table scraps, and he'd happily eat vegetables with a bit of gravy, but she wasn't sure how he would feel about blackberries. She crouched down and offered him a handful, and he sniffed at them, and looked at her uncertainly.

"They're nice," Molly said coaxingly. "Try them, go on."

But he only sniffed again, and licked her fingers, and turned away.

"There isn't anything else," Molly protested. "There really isn't. Oh, Bertie."

Perhaps he'd eat them when he was hungrier, she thought, going back to picking berries for herself. The bush was covered, but she wondered how long all those berries would last her. Should she stop eating, and save them for the next day?

Molly had been trying not to think about where she was going to sleep. But then blackberries for breakfast meant she had to. Was there – would there be a cave, or something like that? She was remembering the story of the Swiss Family Robinson, those children who had been shipwrecked, or bits of it. To be honest she had dozed through a lot of it when Miss read the story out to them. But she was almost sure they'd lived in a cave for a while. Or a tree. There *was* a tree, a big one, out in the middle of the field on the other side of the blackberries. Could she sleep in that? It wasn't even anywhere near dark, but she'd been up so early – she was tired enough to sleep.

The field was laid to grass, but it was empty, thankfully. The sheep had been big enough, and the cows she had seen from the train looked even larger. Molly fought and wriggled her way through the brambles and the broken-down gate, and plodded wearily across the field to look at the tree. She liked the idea of being off the ground, just in case, though she wasn't sure in case of what. She'd never climbed a tree, but it couldn't be that hard.

Even someone who knew nothing about the countryside or trees could see that this one was something special. It was massive. So huge that Molly reckoned she and Vicky and all the other girls who'd been in the train compartment might reach round it if they held hands. It had been climbed a lot before, she could tell – there were patches on the bark worn smooth where feet had scrabbled. A thick rope had been tied around one of the branches, like a swing. And even better, someone had laid two boards in a fork of the branches and nailed them down. They made a tiny platform, nestled in between the massive branches. It looked safe, and almost cosy.

Bertie was a lot less keen on the idea than Molly was. She was sure that if he tried, he could actually leap up to where the tree trunk divided, but he flatly refused, even when Molly climbed up and called to him. So she dragged up the case and her coat, and then went back down to lift him, kicking and wriggling, up into the tree. "You have to," she muttered as he whined and scrabbled. "Ow! Stop scratching at me. Do you want to be eaten by a – by a wolf?" She wouldn't be at all surprised out here. "There!" She sat down on the little platform, stroking Bertie over and over and murmuring to him until he calmed down. But even though he was sitting still, he was still making tiny yipping noises as he looked down at the grass below. Molly could feel him quivering, as though he was about to make a jump for the ground.

"If you stay," she whispered, "I promise I'll find you something better to eat tomorrow. Something you'll actually like. Like those bone biscuits. I promise."

Bertie kept whining for a while, but eventually, as it started to get dark, he seemed to settle, curling up with Molly on top of her coat. She was glad of the warmth – the heat of the day seemed to die away so quickly. There were odd noises too, more and more of them as it grew darker, squeaks and rustling in the grass, and then a rasping shriek that made Molly jump so much she nearly fell out of the tree.

Bertie sat up at that one, peering intently out into the grey evening.

"What was it?" Molly asked shakily. She hadn't really meant it about the wolves, but that noise could have been one. It could have been all sorts of things. Then she clutched at Bertie in panic as the sound came again, and then a pale shadow drifted past a few feet away. It was so quiet that Molly would have thought she'd just imagined it, except that Bertie was whining with excitement and pawing at the boards.

"That wasn't a ghost, was it?" Molly peered out into the darkness. "Can dogs see ghosts? Come back down, Bertie, come on." She curled up on the coat again, and Bertie padded reluctantly back to her, and snuggled in the crook of her knees.

They lay listening to the night sounds, with Molly shivering and jumping, and Bertie springing up every so often to investigate. But by the time the owl came back, and settled into a dark hole further up the tree, they were both asleep.

The next morning, Molly woke up to find that Bertie was gone. She searched for him in a panic, looking under her coat, behind the case, where she could clearly see there was no dog. He'd run off.

Perhaps he was trying to go back home? Dogs did that, she'd seen a story in the newspaper.

Then she heard a happy snuffling around the trunk of the tree, and Bertie trotted back, lead trailing. He'd clearly been digging for something – there was earth all up his muzzle and staining his white paws – and he looked quite happy.

"What did you eat?" Molly asked him sternly, and he wagged his tail at her. "I hope you're not sick." It did mean she could go and eat blackberries without feeling too guilty about him. She had promised him proper food, though, and they did still have all that money she'd taken from Mum's housekeeping.

Besides, blackberries didn't seem quite so filling this morning, when Molly was tired and cold and her bones ached, and her shoes and socks were soaked from the dew on the grass. She wanted porridge, or at least bread and marge. If they walked to a village with a shop she could hide her case, and just say that she was an evacuee and she'd been sent out to do the shopping. She tried to dampen her handkerchief in the wet grass and wipe around her mouth and get the purplish stains off her fingers, but it didn't work very well. The shop would just have to think that she was scruffy.

It seemed to take a lot longer to get all the way down the track than it had the day before, but eventually she came to the road, and the signpost. The village to the left seemed only to be one mile away, though, so she plumped for that one, and walked on, stopping every so often to swap over the case and Bertie's lead, because the handle was giving her blisters.

They had sped by a few villages on the train the day before, but Molly still found it odd, going from fields to houses. There was hardly even a street, she thought critically – and she was in the village before she'd realized that this was it. She'd left it too late to hide her case under a hedge as she'd meant to, but there didn't seem to be anyone around, so she left it outside the shop window, with Bertie tied to a metal ring on the wall next to it. Then she padded cautiously in with her hand tucked tightly around the shillings in her pocket. The shop seemed to sell almost everything – envelopes and knitted gloves and jars of jam all mixed up together on the shelves. Her mum wouldn't have approved at all. There was even a post office counter squeezed in at the back.

"And what are you looking for, dear?"

Molly jumped. She had thought she was alone in the shop – that the owner was out in the stockroom, which wasn't good, because Mum said you couldn't trust anyone. But she hadn't seen that there was a stool behind the counter, and a tiny, elderly lady was peering at her. She was only just tall enough to see over the top.

"Dog biscuits," Molly squeaked. "Um, and plain biscuits too, please. Do you have bags of broken ones?" She had meant to buy bread, but there wasn't any on the shelves. There was probably a baker's elsewhere in the village, but she didn't want to risk staying any longer to find it.

"Dog biscuits. . ." The little old woman shook her head. "Not much call for those here, dear. London ways. . . A bit of bread and milk, much better."

"Oh. . ." Molly rubbed one of her cardigan buttons round and round while she tried to think. "What about the plain biscuits?"

"Yes, yes, we've got those. Twopence for a big paper bag of the broken ones, dear. From London, are you? Did you come on that motorbus the other day?"

"Yes," Molly lied firmly.

"And who are you staying with, dear?"

"A lady. . ." Molly kept her voice vague. "Down the road. Auntie Gladys, she said to call her."

"Gladys. . ." The old woman frowned, tapping her fingers on the counter. She had huge swollen knuckles, Molly noticed, they made her fingers look like gnarled old sticks. "Now where would that be? Down Fletcher's Row, perhaps?"

"Can I have two bags, please?" Molly said, ignoring her and dumping the two bags of biscuits on the counter. Two bags would keep her and Bertie going a couple of days, she reckoned, if she ate blackberries too, and maybe apples, if they found a tree. She had to make her money last.

The old woman counted out the change with agonizing slowness, still trying to work out where Molly was staying, while Molly nodded, and said she didn't know, and said she didn't know again, and tried not to hop from foot to foot. At last the coins were counted into her hand, and she gathered up the biscuits and darted out to shove them into her little case. Bertie could smell them, and he jumped up at her over and over, trying to snap at the paper bags, but Molly got them packed away at last, only to find the old woman staring at her from the door.

"Funny sort of shopping bag," she said, eyeing Molly's case with her head on one side.

Molly looked at her, and at her swollen joints, and decided it was safe enough just to run.

*

She was more careful the next time. When she saw the first houses at the edge of a village, she hid her suitcase, and walked in just with Bertie. She tried tying him to a fence and leaving him too, thinking that she'd be less noticeable without a dog, but he seemed to think that this was different from being left outside a shop, and he whined and howled and pulled at his lead as she walked away, and in the end she ran back to fetch him before he hurt himself.

No one chased after her, not in any of the villages she walked by. But she was getting grubbier. Her blue dress was stained with greenish streaks from climbing the tree that first evening, and she'd slipped over in a lane that had been all churned up by cows when she was wearing the pink gingham dress she'd packed. There was still blackberry under her nails, and her hair smelled. She'd brought a comb, but she hadn't washed properly for days now. She'd tried scrubbing her feet and washing her hands and face and hair in a little stream, but the cold water didn't seem to have done much good, and she'd got gritty mud in her hair when she tried to dip her head in. Her socks had never dried properly either, and she hadn't dared try washing the cresses.

Halfway through the second week, she caught two ladies chatting outside a village shop eyeing her disgustedly, and glared back at them. But then she saw herself reflected in the shop window, and thought that Mum and Stella would have said exactly the same. Bertie was cleaner than she was. And that was after she'd tried to tidy herself up.

"Really, who's that one staying with? I mean, I know they came with hardly anything, but it's no excuse. She's filthy."

"Oh, I know, Moira, but honestly, it's very difficult if they just haven't been taught clean habits. One of the little boys next door to us, you won't believe me, but. . ." Then she saw that Molly was listening, and turned away to whisper.

Molly spent a while in the shop looking at

soap, but it seemed expensive for someone who had eight shillings and sixpence to last her the rest of the war. She didn't want to admit to herself that she was waiting until the gossipy women had left, so she didn't have to walk past them again.

She rubbed the coins in her coat pocket as she and Bertie walked back to where she'd stashed her case. She'd seen a tumbledown barn on the way into the village, and she was planning to spend the night there. There might be straw bales to sleep on. There would be rats, but she had seen them before at home – even in the kitchen, once – and Bertie was proving very useful at scaring them away. He didn't seem to want to eat them, though, which was a pity, because Molly was pretty sure that sweet biscuits weren't good for him. She couldn't afford to buy him meat, and how was she supposed to make porridge, or gravy?

She pulled her case out from under the hedge, and put the biscuits away inside without eating any. She was hungry, but she was getting rather tired of bread and biscuits. Still, they were the cheapest thing that didn't need cooking.

"Come on then," she murmured to Bertie. "You can go ratting. You'll like that. Oh, wait." There was someone coming, she could hear hooves clopping, and the jingle of a harness. Molly glanced around anxiously. There was nowhere to hide, except in the damp little ditch under the hedge where she'd put her case. Miserably, she crouched down and huddled into it, feeling the wet seep into her shoes where the soles were coming loose. That would be more mud stains on her coat, she thought, hauling Bertie after her.

Crouching in the mud, trying to hold back Bertie, who was desperate to chase after the cart and bark at the horse, Molly wondered what she was going to do next. The money wasn't going to last for ever. She had considered just taking that soap – she needed it, after all! And it was only one bar… But so many times she'd heard her mum and Stella talking about people who stole from the shop. How it was taking the food out of the mouths of hard-working people. She'd already taken the money, that was bad enough, and it was from her own family. It would be much worse to steal from strangers. She had taken the blackberries too, though she was almost sure that they didn't belong to anyone. She was less sure about the apples she'd picked from a tree leaning over a garden wall. She found herself peering in now, as she walked past cottage gardens. There was washing on lines, and once she'd seen a loaf of bread cooling on a windowsill. She could have been in and out, so quickly. . .

What was she going to do? Wearily, she dragged herself up out of the ditch, and tried to squeeze out the hem of her coat. It wasn't just wet, she realized miserably. There must have been something rotten in that ditch. She smelled worse than ever.

She was tired from waking up in a panic so many times every night. With each rustle in the grass, she expected wolves or man-eating rats or the police coming to take her back. She was dirty, and her feet were blistered, and she was desperately, desperately lonely, even with Bertie. The shop assistants were the only people she'd spoken to for the last four days.

She kept remembering that broadcast on Sunday. Less than two weeks ago, the first day of the war. *Keep off the streets as much as possible. To expose yourself unnecessarily adds to your danger.* That had been meant for everywhere, not just London. And here she was, ignoring it completely. She was just wandering, and she didn't even know where she was going. She didn't think there had been bombs or gas, not yet. Surely the two busybodies outside that last village shop would have said something, if there had been? The newspaper she had seen in the shop had headlines about the premier flying to France, and mines being laid under the streets of Warsaw. Molly didn't know where that was, but it wasn't anywhere close. No mention of any attacks in England.

Any day now, though, the bombs were going to start falling. And the box for her gas mask was getting dirty, and worn. What if it was damaged, and it didn't work?

She wanted to go home, but she was afraid to.

What was she going to do?

Chapter Eight

The barn was even more tumbledown than it had looked from the road. There was a rusty padlock and chain around the huge main doors, but there were so many holes in the wood that it made no difference. Molly and Bertie squeezed through a rotting gap, and into the building. It was quite dark inside already, and Molly stood for a while, trying to let her eyes adjust. The barn smelled musty, and she could hear scurrying feet. It was mostly dry, though, if she avoided the holes in the roof. Eventually she was able to make out a ladder leading up to another floor at one end of the barn, with what looked like straw piled up. It would be more comfortable to sleep up there, and she'd feel safer, as long as the ladder was still holding together. Molly shook it gently, and nothing came off in her hand. She began to climb up, leaving Bertie on the ground to go sniffing after rats.

"I'll bring you up if the floor's not full of holes," she called down to him. But the wooden boards seemed quite solid, and there were piles of hay that still had a faint sweet smell to them. The roof had held together better in this part of the building. Molly gathered up the hay into a mound and laid her coat down on top. It was almost luxury. Perhaps she could stay here, she wondered for a moment, thinking of setting up her own tiny home. But it wouldn't work. She couldn't keep going back to the same shops without people starting to ask questions.

Her bright mood died away again, and she lay down on her hay bed, gazing up at the shadows of the ceiling and thinking that there would probably be bats. She was half dozing when she heard Bertie whining at the bottom of the ladder, and she got up yawning to fetch him and feed him a handful of the biscuits she'd bought. He didn't seem to mind the boring diet at all, gobbling them up and licking her fingers eagerly. Molly tried not to think of all the times Mum had made her wash her hands because she'd been playing with him. She rubbed her hands on her skirt before she ate her own share.

"We're all right, aren't we?" she whispered to Bertie as he wriggled on to her pile of hay and turned himself round and round a few times. "We were right to come away, weren't we? It's just..." She ran out of words. "I don't know. I thought it would be ... easier."

Something flew by overhead, and Molly turned sideways, curling herself around Bertie and trying not to think about bats getting caught in her hair. They hadn't come anywhere near her so far, but she had seen them in the films. Perhaps they only liked clean film star hair, she thought sleepily. She was far too grubby now. . .

"Rose, come on. Get in here. It's raining, come on. There aren't any rats, I promise."

Molly blinked to herself, and yawned, listening to the voices. Someone talking in the yard under her window, she thought, scratching idly at an itchy spot on her leg. Hay was good to sleep on, except it was so tickly.

Then she woke up properly, and remembered where she was. There was someone else in the barn! Very, very slowly, she sat up, putting her hand round Bertie's muzzle. He stared at her and tried to shake her hand away, but Molly pressed her finger to her lips hopefully. She'd never tried to train him to be quiet, but surely he was clever enough to work it out? "Ssshh. . ." she breathed. And Bertie shot backwards, dashed round her and stood at the edge of the hayloft, barking his loudest watchdog bark.

She was up at the top of a ladder, Molly thought. She couldn't run. Then again, the voice had sounded quite young. A boy, she reckoned, and not much older than her. Perhaps she could just kick him in the shins and run if he tried to catch her. Why would he, anyway, she told herself. Unless the barn belonged to his family, or something like that, she had just as much right to be here as he did.

She crouched down at the edge of the platform and leaned over to look.

Standing in the middle of the barn, staring up at her in horror, were a boy and a girl, who looked about as scruffy and unloved as Molly did.

"Who are you?" the boy demanded. The smaller girl didn't say anything. She just watched, her eyes dark and round in a pale, dirt-smudged face. Her dress was pink gingham, like Molly's spare, and it was filthy.

"Mind your own business," Molly snapped. She was trying to work out how to get down there with Bertie and her case, without leaving anything at the bottom of the ladder for these two to nick. They looked desperate enough. Then she nearly sniggered. They were probably thinking exactly the same about her.

"Bertie, come on," she muttered, picking him up and tucking him under her arm. Then she started backwards down the ladder. She could feel the two children's eyes on her back. Bertie scrambled out of her arms halfway down and made a leap for the ground, but he stayed at the bottom of the ladder instead of going to greet them. A few days of running and hiding had made him nervous, Molly realized, as she scurried back up to fetch her case.

"We're just coming in to get out of the rain," the boy said as she climbed back down. He was trying to sound stern, Molly thought, but his eyes were flicking from side to side, as though he was waiting to be jumped on. The little girl was clinging so tightly to his hand that Molly could see him twitching his fingers to stop it hurting.

"So? Doesn't bother me," she said, shrugging. "We're going anyway." But trying to watch them and talk and climb down at the same time meant that she slipped two rungs from the bottom, and dropped the case while she was grabbing on to the ladder. It bounced down and sprang open, spilling Molly's damp socks and spare dress and the biscuits over the earth floor.

"Oh, drat it. Don't you touch that!" she yelled. "It's mine." She jumped down and started to gather up her things. The biscuits hadn't gone on to the floor, luckily, there were just a few of them scattered on the lid of the case. She scrabbled them back into the bag, pushing Bertie away. "In a bit," she muttered to him.

"We weren't going to," the boy said loftily, but the little girl moaned, looking at the biscuits, and Molly looked up at her in surprise. Her face was almost desperate, but she didn't come a step closer.

Molly glanced over at the boy, and saw him grimacing. Fear, maybe? Hunger? He seemed almost ashamed. Then he saw Molly watching him. He wrapped his other arm tightly around the little girl and glared back.

Molly sighed. She could spare a couple of biscuits for someone who looked at them like that. "Do you want one?" she asked the small girl.

She didn't answer, just kept staring at the bag, and Molly turned back to the boy.

"Doesn't she talk?"

"No," he said coldly. "And we don't want your stuff. Go away."

This time, the little girl pulled on his arm and looked up at him pleadingly.

"She does," Molly said, smirking a little.

"Go away!" he yelled. "Leave us alone."

Molly had been meaning to go, but she wasn't letting him talk to her like that. "You go away, I was here first. This is my place." She took two biggish bits of biscuit from the bag and held them out to the little girl. "Here. You can have those."

The girl looked up at her brother, then she

reached out and snatched the biscuits, stuffing one of them into her mouth.

"Rose!" he hissed. "You can't take that. Give it back!"

"Too late." Molly shrugged. "I've got enough." It felt good, being better off than someone else. Really good. She took out another piece and ate it herself, and then fed two bits to Bertie, who was sitting at her feet whining and thumping his tail on the ground.

"Want some then?" she asked the boy after that, and he stared at his feet for a moment and muttered, "Yes. All right then. Please."

Molly handed him some biscuit, and they all ate silently for a moment, watching each other cautiously. The little girl – Rose – wasn't just dirty, Molly realized. The side of her face was bruised, her whole jaw discoloured and puffy. Molly edged back a little. "Did you do that to her?" she asked, nodding towards the little girl.

"No!"

Molly stepped back even further as she saw him clench his fists. "All right! Only asking." She eyed him cautiously. He didn't look like a fighter. He was thin and serious-faced, and his dark hair was too long, falling in his eyes. Boys' clothes didn't show the dirt quite so badly, Molly decided. He had grey shorts on, and one of those knitted pullovers on under his blazer, greyish wool knitted in a pattern that hid the stains. Now she looked carefully, his nails were black, and so were his knees.

"Are you running away, then?" she asked curiously. She wanted to know, now. After four days of talking to Bertie, she was desperate to talk to someone who could answer back. Even if they didn't want to talk to her.

"What's it to you?"

Molly shrugged. "Nothing. Just wondered. Since you're eating my biscuits."

He hesitated, and then glanced down at his little sister. "Will you give us some more then, if I tell you?"

Was their story worth it? Molly wondered. She could buy more biscuits, but she didn't have that much money. She couldn't waste it. It was just that it was so good to have a little company. She didn't want to go off on her own in a huff. Or make the bruised, silent little girl go out in the rain.

"I'll see," she hedged. She sat down on the bottom rung of the ladder to the hayloft. "Go on then. What are you doing out here?" She blinked, hit by a sudden worry. "You haven't been bombed? They haven't started sending planes over?"

"No. Nothing yet. My father said it would be any day, but I haven't seen a single plane." He sounded disappointed for a moment.

"So what *are* you doing here?"

He sighed and sat down on a pile of old sacks, pulling his sister down next to him. "You're right. We're running away." He glanced up. "I suppose you are too."

"I might be," Molly admitted. "You first."

"Only if you give us the biscuits."

Molly sighed loudly. "All right! Here." She dug into the bag and gave him a handful, and a couple to Bertie, who was nudging at her hopefully.

"We were evacuated from London. And we didn't like it so we're running away. There."

"You can give me those back," Molly growled. "That's no story at all."

The little girl started to cram the biscuits into her mouth so quickly she was in danger of choking, and her brother pulled at her hand. "Stop it, Rose. Don't do that, I'll tell her properly."

"You'd better," Molly said warningly. "Or I won't give you another crumb. And you can go out in the rain for all I care."

Rose elbowed her brother hard, and he shook her off grumpily. She obviously understood what was going on, Molly thought. So was it that she couldn't talk, or she wouldn't?

"I'm getting to it, Rose. I'm just trying to think where to start. All right. Our grandma died. A month ago?" He glanced at Rose uncertainly, and started to count back on his fingers. "Yes. A month ago. And she'd looked after us for ages. Years and years. Our mum died of TB when Rose was three. So it was us and Dad and Gran, you see?"

Molly nodded.

"Then we didn't have Gran any more, and there was no one around to look after us, and it was the summer so there was no school. And Rose wouldn't stop crying." Rose elbowed him again and he shot sideways, rubbing his ribs and scowling at her. "It's true! All right, I cried too. Anyway. Dad didn't know what to do. He got one of the neighbours to watch us with her kids, but there wasn't a lot of room round hers. Ronnie and Carol are younger, as well. It wasn't working out. I suppose we might have moaned." He picked at a scratch on his knee, and then looked up angrily at Molly. "It was like he just wanted to get rid of us! He didn't even talk to us about going, he signed us up, and then he told it was happening and we didn't have a word to say about it."

Molly could hear the anger in his voice, and the hurt. "But if he wanted you to be safe," she tried to say, but the boy shook his head angrily.

"It wasn't that. He just saw his chance to have us out of his way."

Molly nodded. Their father seemed to be the opposite of her mum. "So did you get sent away on that Friday?"

"Yeah. On a bus out here to Essex. A village." He snorted. "They kept talking about us as if we were poor little London kids who didn't know anything. There were some cottages in that village that didn't even have water laid on. But the place we got sent to did." He ducked his head. "That was about the only good thing about it." He was silent for a minute. "Look, we're not stupid. We tried. I knew Dad wouldn't want us back, we did try. But – Rose had lost her gran, and she didn't know what was happening, and everything was strange."

Molly glanced at the little girl, and saw that she'd gone bright red. She wriggled round on the pile of sacks so that she wasn't facing Molly any more.

"She – er – she disgraced herself," her brother muttered.

"What does that mean?" Molly asked, frowning. Mum had called Pearl next door a disgrace for her bad language and fancy clothes. "Did she swear?"

"No!" The boy half laughed. "No, she wet the bed."

"Oh. . ."

"There were three kids there and they kept teasing Rose. Calling her a baby, and – other stuff. Much worse than that. Then one of the girls took her toy cat and said Rose gave it to her. Rose wasn't talking much then, but she did say a bit, and she told their mother, but Mrs Kemp called her a liar." Molly saw his fingers clench into fists. "Why would she give that little horror her cat? It was like the only thing she had! And then when she wet the bed Mrs Kemp rubbed her face in the sheets."

Rose made a strange little moaning noise again, and he reached round to hold her. "She made us wash them. And then when Rose did it again, she hit her."

Molly stared at him. She hadn't been sure whether to believe him before, when he said it wasn't him that had given his little sister that bruise. She didn't have any brothers or sisters close to her own age, of course. Stella was so much older that sometimes Molly felt like an only child. All the brothers and sisters she knew fought with each other, though. She'd thought he was just trying to cover it up. But for a grown woman to hit a little girl in the face, hard enough to bruise. . . Her mum had smacked her, but not very often, and never, never that hard.

"And she said Rose would get it worse next time. That's when we left."

Rose turned herself back round and held something out to Molly. A tiny stuffed cat, made of pale brown felt. It had green bead eyes, and a bow sewn up out of a scrap of the same pink checked gingham that Rose's dress was made from. Molly guessed that their gran had made the dress, and the little cat too.

"You got it back!" Molly dug her nails into her palms. The toy reminded her of Tom again. It was almost exactly the colour of the stripes on his fat sausage tail.

"She stole it out of Nora's coat pocket. Nearly got us caught." He rolled his eyes, but Molly thought he sounded a little bit admiring.

"What's your name?" she asked suddenly. It didn't seem right, listening to this story without knowing it.

He hesitated, but only for a moment. "John."

"I'm Molly."

They nodded to each other, a bit embarrassed, and Molly folded her arms. "Go on, then. What happened next? You just set off walking?"

"We couldn't pack properly." He shot an envious glance at Molly's case. "They'd put our bags away in a cupboard – one of the kids would have told on us if we'd tried to get them. They followed us around all the time to pick on us, never left us alone. So all we've got's that cat and our gas masks and the clothes we had on. We were supposed to be on our way home from school. Nora and Jack and Ellen went off with some of the others – so we walked the other way." He shrugged. "I couldn't see a better time to do it. We're not going back either, however bad it gets." He glared at Molly, as if he thought she might try and persuade them. "God knows what they'd do to us."

"Why didn't you write to your dad, though?" Molly asked. "I know you said he wanted you gone, but I bet he wouldn't have wanted them hitting Rose."

"I did that," he told her quietly.

"And he didn't let you come home?" Molly said uncomfortably. She hadn't meant to make things worse.

"I wrote to him – I had to, I told him the state Rose was in. How she stopped talking – and she used to talk nineteen to the dozen." He looked down at his little sister, half anxious, half exasperated. "He came to visit us, that weekend. He got a train out, and then a lift on a cart, and he turned up on the Saturday afternoon." Rose snuggled closer to him, and he closed his eyes before he went on with the story. "Mrs Kemp said we were lying. She told him about Rose wetting the bed, and said that of course Rose was missing Gran and she was doing her best to look after her. Then she sighed and went on about how much work washing all the sheets made. And then she said – she said our gran must have spoiled Rose, because she didn't like living with another little girl, and she picked fights with Nora. She told him Rose broke Nora's doll on purpose so she'd said Rose had to give her the cat. It was all lies," he added earnestly. "All of it! Rose isn't spoiled! My gran was really strict. Everyone in our road knew it, but they said it was worth it because she was such a good cook."

"He believed her instead of you, then?"

John nodded, looking sick. "He said he was

ashamed of us behaving so badly, and we weren't to write such lies again. And he gave Mrs Kemp five shillings, for having to do all that extra washing. You should have seen her, when Mr Kemp took him back to the station in the pony trap. The face on her – like a cat with ten gallons of cream. She knew she could do anything now. And our dad would send her more money if she whined enough."

"I'm sorry," Molly whispered. At least her mum had wanted her around, she thought, feeling guilty.

"So, what's your story?" He sat back, hugging Rose tight.

"I never got evacuated. My mum didn't believe in it." She was picking her words carefully, trying not to let them think she was gloating about a mother who wanted to keep her at home. "I had to run because of him. Bertie, this is Bertie." Bertie looked up, and came trotting back over. He'd been sniffing hopefully round the edges of the barn, looking for rats. "He's friendly, it's just that we've been hiding from people so I think he's confused."

Rose wriggled out of John's arm and crouched down, whispering hopefully to Bertie. The dog looked over at Molly, and then licked Rose's hand, making her laugh delightedly and scuttle back to her brother. But she kept watching Bertie, clearly longing to do it again.

"You can stroke him," Molly told her. "Go on. It's all right." She looked at John. "You see? He's a good dog. Really friendly."

"Why does that mean you had to run away?" he asked. "I don't see. . ."

"There was this big fuss about dogs being scared of the bombs. A whole line of people round us – there must have been fifty of them? Maybe even more. They took their dogs to the vet to be destroyed. Cats as well."

"But what for?"

Molly shrugged. "I don't really know. It doesn't make that much sense. Everyone was so scared about being bombed. People were in a panic, weren't they? Running around like headless chickens sorting the blackout blinds and worrying about the shelters. Did you know there was an air raid siren straight after Mr Chamberlain's broadcast saying we were at war? You'd have been gone by then." She closed her eyes, looking back through the days, through all that walking. "There was a lady running down our street shrieking. I'd forgotten. My mum thought Bertie would be sent mad by the bombs. That's what she said. But I think—" She swallowed hard. "I think it was more like getting rid of everything that didn't really matter. Because no one knew what was going to happen."

"So you left before she could do it?"

"Yes." And then, because John had told her how his dad had betrayed them, she explained what she hadn't brought herself to admit to the girls on the train. "I left our Tom, though. Our cat. He jumped out of the basket when I was walking to the station. She was going to take him to be put to sleep too, but I had to leave him. I couldn't get him back."

Rose's eyes went rounder and even darker, and she pressed her little ginger-brown cat tight under her chin. Molly looked away, ashamed. "I don't know what happened to him." She fiddled with the buttons on her cardigan so as not to look at John and Rose, and then jumped as someone put their arms around her. Rose was clinging on around her neck. No one had held Molly since she'd crept out of the bed she shared with Stella, a week and a half before. She sat like a statue, not wanting to move in case Rose let go.

Chapter Nine

Molly discovered over the next few weeks that having someone to talk to wasn't the only benefit of travelling in a group. As the nights grew colder, huddling together in the barns and sheds and – once – under a cricket pavilion, was very welcome. She and John curled up on either side of Rose, and Bertie usually slept on top of all of them. Rose and John had been set to work while they were staying with the Kemps, feeding the chickens and collecting eggs, and they were good at it. Chickens didn't always lay where they were meant to,

John explained to Molly. Hunting around near a henhouse often meant an egg or two. Molly would have thought that was no use at all – she wasn't going to eat a raw egg – but John had been a Wolf Cub, and knew about lighting fires and campfire cooking. He showed her how to bake eggs in the ashes once a fire was dying down.

He was also a great deal less worried about stealing than Molly was. As John saw it, someone was supposed to be looking after the three of them, but no one actually was. So they were looking after themselves, and sometimes that meant they had to take things. He explained it to Molly and Rose very determinedly, and it made sense, when he was talking. In the middle of the night, Molly wasn't so sure, but she was hungry enough to tell herself it was right.

They were all getting hungrier, and colder. The weather changed at the beginning of October, and the warm, sunny September days when it wasn't too much of a hardship to be outside disappeared.

It began to rain instead, heavy, drenching downpours that meant they got wet and stayed wet. Bertie's paws were so permanently soaked that they turned pink and tender under the dirt, and he hobbled. Molly's shoes fell apart, so she had to wear her plimsolls, which meant her feet never dried either.

Molly spent her money very carefully, just a penny or so on biscuits or bread here and there, and while she was paying, Rose would slip a box of matches up her sleeve. But they were so battered and grubby-looking now that as soon as they walked into a shop, they were watched. Molly realized that her mother probably wouldn't even have let her in. Or at least Stella would have been following her around the shelves keeping an eye on her.

Gardens were easier, if they watched carefully to make sure everyone was inside. They were living mostly on stolen eggs and fruit. Rose insisted on taking a marrow, once. It was huge – there was an even larger one, but it would have been too big to carry, and John said it wouldn't be fair anyway, to take the prize marrow. Molly had tried to argue that they didn't know what to do with a marrow, but John said they could toast chunks of it over the fire on sticks. Mostly they took it because Rose was exhausted and wet and miserable and she wanted a marrow. She trailed behind them with it cradled in her arms like a baby, and she wept again when John cut bits off it with his penknife. It didn't toast very well, but they ate it anyway.

As autumn went on, it was getting harder and harder to find anything to steal. Almost everyone had picked the apples and plums off their trees. A few vegetable patches had carrots, or runner beans, but pickings were thin. There were hardly any blackberries left either, and Molly was down to her last two shillings.

Finding a garden with a laden apple tree, and what looked like a weedy overgrown sort of vegetable patch, meant that for the first time in days they might not go to sleep hungry. There was someone in it when they walked past. Even though it was raining, she was sitting in a deckchair gazing down the lawn towards the apple tree at the end. Molly peered round the gate in the wall to look in, and the woman was sitting so still that at first Molly didn't see her. She was about to point out the vegetable patch to John and Rose when John put his hand over her mouth and gestured fiercely at the deckchair, and the feet in the grass below it.

"We can wait and come back," Molly whispered. "Did you see all those apples? And I expect there were carrots." She recognized the feathery tops now. Carrots were sweet enough to eat raw, and they were more filling than apples. The three children walked on along the length of the old wall around the garden, and slipped into the small copse of trees just beyond. They waited under the dripping trees, stamping their feet and huddling their arms around themselves. Rose sat on Molly's case, looking limp.

"She can't stay out there much longer," Molly said hopefully, brushing her wet hair out of her eyes.

"What's she even doing sitting out there in the rain?" John asked. "She's got a house. It looked big, too. Big garden."

"Maybe she just likes being in the rain?" Molly suggested, but she sounded doubtful. None of them could imagine liking rain now, not after the last few days. Who would get wet when they didn't have to?

"I'm going to climb up and look," John said eventually. "That old wall's got footholds in it, I can get up there."

"She'll see you!"

"Not if I only put my head over the top a minute." He took off his wet coat – it wasn't doing him a lot of good anyway – and ran at the wall, leaping up and grabbing at a place where the mortar was falling out. He scrambled up, and got an arm over the top, peering over cautiously. "She's gone!" he hissed back. "At least, the deckchair's empty now. It's a bit hard to see, the trees are in the way. I can't see her in the garden anywhere." He hauled himself up, sitting with one leg either side of the wall. "No, I'm sure she's gone. There's no one here. I'll go and get what I can out of the veg garden."

"Wait," Molly started to say — she was wondering if they should wait until later on, when it was getting dark. But John was already swinging himself over the wall — she could only see his pale fingertips clinging on now.

She and Rose stood by the wall, listening for a scrabble and a thump as he landed in the grass. But instead there was a scraping and a cry, and then a crash of breaking glass.

"What happened?" Molly yelped, and Rose let out a wail of fright. Bertie stood up on his hind paws, his front feet on the wall, whining anxiously.

There was no sound from the other side of the wall. Molly stared at the bricks, and the little clumps of cushiony moss growing in between them, and then down at Rose. "Give me a hand up," she said at last. "He – he must have fallen. . . We'd better see."

Rose linked her hands, and Molly stepped up on to them. Rose was so much littler though, Molly could feel her wobbling. She wouldn't be able to hold Molly's weight for long. Molly caught at the top of the wall and heaved herself up, scraping her arms as she struggled to see over the top.

John was just underneath her at the other side of the wall, lying silent and half-curled. He had fallen into the long, untidy grass at the end of the garden, between a compost heap and an elderly wheelbarrow with a hole in. Molly couldn't tell what it was he'd fallen in – some sort of glass and wooden thing. She supposed it had been left at the end of the garden because it was broken. She hoped it had been, anyway, because it was certainly broken now.

"John! John!" she hissed. "Are you all right? Are you hurt?" She knew it was a stupid question – of course he was hurt. He looked like he'd knocked himself out. But she couldn't help hoping that he was going to groan and roll over and pick himself up, the way he had when he'd caught his foot on a bit of wire climbing through a fence a few days before.

He didn't.

He stayed still and horribly pale, apart from his dirty grey sock, which was darkening rapidly with blood where the broken glass had gashed him.

Molly wriggled harder, trying to pull herself up so she was properly on top of the wall, the way John had done. But she couldn't do it. Her arms just didn't seem to work that way – she was having a hard enough time staying where she was. She let go with a gasp and dropped back down next to Rose, landing in a heap.

"He fell on something," she tried to explain. She didn't want to terrify John's little sister, but Rose had to know. "He's cut his leg. I can't get over that wall, Rose. I think we might have to go in round by the gate."

192

Rose looked shocked. They had to stay hidden, they both knew that.

"We have to! I think he banged his head too, he's not moving. We have to go and help him, even if it does mean we get caught."

She had thought Rose was pale before, but now all the colour faded out of the little girl's face, leaving just the dirt and the last yellowish remnants of her bruise.

"You won't have to go back to them," Molly told her fiercely. "You won't, I promise. None of us has anything that says who we are, and we're not telling. You don't talk anyway! Nobody's going to know where you came from. Come on." She grabbed Rose's hand, and they ran around the corner of the walled garden to the wooden gate, still standing open. Molly only stopped for a second to peer in. It didn't matter if there was someone in the garden, she realized. They had to go in anyway.

Bertie dashed ahead as Molly dragged Rose after

her past long flower beds, mostly seed heads and dead stems now, and a little arbour with plants growing up to shade a bench. The formal part of the garden gave way to the vegetable patch, and then at last a shed that hid the compost heap and the rubbish pile where John was lying.

He hadn't moved at all – he was still slumped in the wreckage of the glass thing, a cold frame, Molly remembered it was now. They had looked inside one a few days before to see if there was anything they could take. It was like a little greenhouse.

Rose crouched down beside him, patting his face, but he didn't move, and she looked back at Molly in anguish.

"I think he needs a hospital," Molly said, turning to look back up the garden. The house at the end was huge, and dark. No windows seemed to be lit, even though it was such a gloomy afternoon. Perhaps they'd put their blackout up already? "Stay here with him," she told Rose. "If he wakes up, tell him everything's going to be all right. Bertie, stay."

She was halfway up the garden before she realized that Rose couldn't tell John anything. But perhaps she would, for this.

Molly knocked on the back door, softly at first – they had spent so long trying to avoid being noticed, it was hard to demand attention. Then harder, until she was slamming at the door with her hands and shouting. But still no one came. Furiously, she rattled the handle, and then half fell into the house as the door opened.

She was in a sort of scullery, off the main kitchen – and the woman who had been sitting in the deckchair was now sitting at the kitchen table and staring at her. She was leaning on the table with her hands over her ears; clearly she had been trying to block out the noise of Molly knocking.

"Go away," she said wearily.

"I can't! We need you to help us. My friend's hurt. He's bleeding, he looks awful and he won't wake up. I think he needs a doctor." Molly hesitated for a moment. They couldn't afford to pay a doctor, but she was desperate.

The tired, locked-up look faded from the woman's face, and she sat up a little. "Bleeding?"

"He fell off the wall on to some glass. We were stealing your apples, I'm sorry. You can call the police, but can't you help him first? He needs a doctor!"

"You'd better show me." She got up, rather clumsily, and pushed her feet into a pair of muddy gardening shoes by the door. Then she glanced around the scullery and picked up a tea towel lying by the sink. "He fell on that broken cold frame? I should have made Peter get rid of it." She leaned on the door frame for a moment, as though she'd lost her breath, and Molly tugged her hand impatiently. "Yes, you should. Please come now!"

When they reached the bottom of the garden, Rose was sitting with John's head cradled in her lap. She'd taken her coat off and put it round him, and she was shivering in her pink gingham dress.

Bertie was sitting beside her, and he thumped his tail in the long wet grass as Molly and the woman came closer.

"What are you children doing here?" the woman asked, staring at Rose in horror. Molly supposed she did look awful, so dirty and ragged.

"We'll go as soon as we can, but I don't know what to do," she gabbled. "Oh! He's waking up!"

"That wasn't what I – never mind." The woman crouched by John and Rose, and took John's hand, rubbing it between her own. "Can you hear me, dear? Look at me."

John was blinking vaguely now, but as he came back to consciousness his eyes flickered between Rose and Molly and the strange woman whose garden they had invaded. He panicked and tried to pull his hand away. He was trying to say something to Rose and Molly but it only came out as a frightened mumble.

"No, keep still," the woman said gently. She wrapped the tea towel she'd picked up around the long cut on John's leg, tying it on loosely. "You're quite badly cut, and there might be glass in this. It's all right. I can help. I did a first aid course at village hall. Bandaging and things, almost everyone did, last year when everything was looking so awful." She shook her head and muttered, "Not now. So silly." She glanced at Molly. "Can you help me lift him up? We need to get him in the house. It's so cold out here. Shock, you know. It's dangerous."

John nearly fainted again as they pulled him up, and he couldn't walk. In the end Molly and the strange woman half carried him up the garden and into a little sitting room just beyond the kitchen, where they laid him on a sofa.

"He'll get blood on your cushions," Molly pointed out, but the woman only nodded, as though it really didn't matter.

"I'll call the doctor," she murmured. "I'm afraid you might need stitches."

"I don't!" John tried to sit up. "We've got to go. We never took anything. I'm sorry I broke that glass. Come on. . ." He reached out to Rose, but she stepped back from him and grabbed Molly's hand. She was only little, but even she could see that they weren't going anywhere.

The woman ignored him, hurrying out and along a passageway, where they heard her talking to the operator at the telephone switchboard.

"What are you doing?" John growled. "What did you two let her see you for, are you stupid?"

"No!" Molly snapped back. "Half a bucket of blood's in your sock, hadn't you noticed? We thought you were dead!"

"Don't be dim. . ." John slumped back against the cushions, his face greying again. Panic and anger had given him a little burst of strength, but now it was gone.

"She's calling a doctor, but we don't have to tell her who we are." Molly frowned. "Rose, when they ask, you'd better say I'm your sister. That's good, because no one who's looking for us would expect three children. If they don't realize who you are, they can't send you back to the Kemps. And they won't split us up if they think we're all related. Yes?"

Rose nodded, and John whispered, "OK. . ."

Molly glanced around the room. Her case was still out by the wall, and even in that, the only thing that might give a clue to who they were was Vicky's label, still carefully tucked behind the torn fabric lining. "Maybe we should have other names – oh, she's coming back." They turned stony faces towards the door as they heard footsteps.

"He was at home, luckily. He'll be here in five minutes or so." The woman sat down on the end of the sofa, looking exhausted, and Molly suddenly realized that she was going to have a baby. She wasn't showing much, but Molly remembered that look on Pearl's mother. That must be why she seemed so tired. But it didn't explain sitting out in the rain.

"So. . ." She rubbed her hands across her face, and then looked thoughtfully at Molly and Rose. Then she nodded, as though she had made a decision. "You two had better go and wash. Quickly."

Molly gaped at her, but Rose jumped up from where she'd been crouching next to John. She looked delighted at the thought of washing.

"In the scullery. There's soap, and the boiler should have hot water. Just – do your best, before the doctor arrives." She looked at John's filthy hands, and sighed. "You might get away with it, being a boy."

"I don't know what she's thinking?" Molly whispered to Rose as they scrubbed their hands in the big china sink. "I suppose maybe the doctor won't treat John if we look like we're poor. I've got two shillings left, though. I don't know... Ugh..." The water was grey and scummy with dirt and soapsuds. "Here, there's another of those cloths. Let me wash your face. At least the rain meant our hair's a bit cleaner." She scrubbed at Rose, trying to rinse away the line of grime along her neck. "Our dresses, though. Oh well. If we had time, I'd wash you too," she added to Bertie, looking admiringly at the sink. "You'd fit in here perfectly."

The doorbell jangled, and the two girls jumped. Molly quickly dragged the cloth over Rose's face again, and they dashed out to the passage. The woman passed them on their way into the room and nodded approvingly. "Much better."

They stood by John's sofa, listening to the voices further down the passage as she explained to the doctor.

"But I didn't realize you had any evacuees, Mrs Tolley, with the way things had been. The vicar's wife said she didn't think it was appropriate to ask you just now."

"These are my cousin's children. From London. She asked me as a favour, you see. I couldn't really say no."

Molly tried not to let her mouth fall open again. The woman – Mrs Tolley – she wasn't giving them up? She was going to lie for them?

"And of course, being London children, I'm

afraid they simply aren't used to playing outside in quite the same way. I just don't know how you managed to do this to yourself," she said to John, who was blinking at her dazedly. "You were supposed to be taking care of your sisters!"

"Accidents happen," the doctor murmured, unwrapping John's leg. "Mmm. Yes, it's not too bad. Seems reasonably clean." He sent Mrs Tolley for hot water and sponged away the drying blood that was caked up John's leg. Now that they weren't in the middle of trying to rescue him any more, Molly discovered that looking at the ugly cut made her feel quite sick. She thought it was being able to see the edges of him. She retreated to the end of the sofa, and left Rose to hold John's hand while the doctor stitched him up and swathed the leg in bandages. Then he left all sorts of instructions about fevers and infection and leaking that only made Molly feel worse. But when Mrs Tolley came back from seeing him out, Molly made herself stand up.

Even though the last few weeks had been

desperately uncertain, she had been relying on herself, and then on herself and John and Rose. They hadn't had to depend on anyone else. Now, she had no idea what was going to happen, and it was unreasonably frightening.

"Why did you lie?" John croaked at her as she came back into the room. The stitches had been painful, and the medicine the doctor had given him to help with the pain hadn't started to work yet. He managed to wriggle up on his elbows, but that was all.

Mrs Tolley shook out the cushion behind his head, fluffing it up so that he could lean back. "I heard your sisters talking. Or – not your sisters? Are any of you actually related?"

Molly and John exchanged frantic glances. What should they say? Was it better to lie? But Mrs Tolley seemed to want to help; what if they only made her angry with them?

"I'm not," Molly said at last. "Rose and John are really brother and sister, but I don't belong. Bertie's mine, though," she added, pointing at him.

Mrs Tolley laughed, a real laugh this time. "Your family is the dog?" she murmured.

Molly shrugged uncomfortably. It sounded awful, said like that. But it was true.

"Yes," she said firmly.

"Have you children been living outside?" Mrs Tolley picked up Rose's abandoned coat, looking at the tear in the back, and the mud all over. "You've been camping? In all this rain?"

"There were barns to sleep in," Molly explained. "Last night we found a garden shed. It even had deckchairs in it."

"But *why*?"

They gazed back at her silently.

"I suppose you can't tell me that," Mrs Tolley said at last. "Because you're frightened that I'll work out who you are, and send you back."

Molly nodded. "Why haven't you got any evacuees already?" she asked. "The doctor said something about them not asking you. Is it because you're having a baby?" She felt herself go pink – that wasn't something you were supposed to ask about. It was something mothers talked over in whispers, while children were sent out of the room. But it mattered. There was something strange about this woman, and this house. John and Rose had suffered enough staying with the Kemps. She wasn't going to let Rose be badly treated again, especially as John was hurt. She had to look after both of them now, as well as Bertie.

Mrs Tolley swallowed, and then opened her mouth as if she was about to speak, and then swallowed again. "Yes. . ." she said slowly, at last. "I'm having a baby. My husband is in the army, he's away, training. I haven't been very well. So Mrs Tennant – the vicar's wife, she's the billeting officer – she told me that they'd left my house off the list. I'm not quite sure how she did it."

"We'll go, as soon as that medicine starts working," John told her, trying to sit up.

"And I've got two shillings you can have, to pay

for the doctor," Molly put in.

"You could stay. If you wanted." She glanced at them sideways. "I was quite looking forward to having the children from London to stay. For the company."

"But – don't you have to find out who we belong to? Won't you get into trouble for keeping us?" Molly was still feeling suspicious.

"I don't see why." Mrs Tolley sighed. "Who knows how long any of us will be here? Half the village wants to tell me how ready the Germans are for war every time I walk down the street. No one knows what's going to happen."

Chapter Ten

It wasn't until two days later that they found out the truth. The girl who came to help Mrs Tolley with the housework, Phyllis, told Molly and Rose while they were drying up for her. By then, the girls' dresses were washed and mended, and Mrs Tolley had gone through some of her brother's old clothes in the loft to find something for John to wear. She said she didn't think they'd ever make his own shorts and shirt look presentable. She'd unravelled his jumper, and promised to knit it over again, as much the same as she could. Clothes were bound to be hard to come by soon, she told them. The three children looked as though they might just about have been sent to Marsh End by Mrs Tolley's London cousin, although Phyllis was shocked by how little they'd been packed off with, and she kept asking Molly questions about her supposed mother. Clearly Phyllis thought that she was neglectful.

"I mean – one dress for you, Rose! What was she thinking?"

"It was all a rush. We weren't going to go, and then she talked to someone and changed her mind," Molly murmured. She was desperately trying to remember what she and John and Rose – and Mrs Tolley – had already told all the people who asked. It was quite hard keeping track of the stories. She'd been right when she told the girls on the train the truth because it was easier. "She knew Auntie Lucy was good at sewing and she could make Rose another one."

Rose looked round, beaming. Mrs Tolley had

found some flowered print fabric in her sewing cupboard, and she'd nearly finished making Rose another dress already. She'd taken Molly's shoes to be mended, too. They had fallen on their feet, John said. Rose had snorted with laughter, pointing at his bandaged leg and then dancing out of his way with a smirk. But he was right – Mrs Tolley, however strange and sad she seemed, was kind, patient and a very good cook. Even Bertie had been bathed in that huge white sink, and Mrs Tolley had found an old brush. He almost gleamed.

"Well, that was true." Phyllis nodded wisely. "Poor Mrs Tolley. She was always the best-dressed lady in the village, you know. Got all those picture papers, and the outfits she could make!"

Molly blinked. Mrs Tolley wore a tweed skirt and a soft woollen jumper, most of the time – they were good quality, Molly could tell, but they weren't enormously stylish. "Is it because of the baby that she's not dressing smart now?" she asked.

Phyllis looked round at her in surprise, her

hands still plunged in the soapy water. "You don't know? Oh. . . Of course you don't." Her face brightened with the treat of telling someone the news. "Her husband. . ."

"Peter." Molly nodded. "He's away training. He's in the army."

"No." Phyllis managed to look sad and smug at the same time. "He isn't. He was killed in an accident. A car hit him, just outside the training camp."

"But Mrs Tolley – Auntie Lucy, I mean – she said he was coming back."

Phyllis leaned over and whispered meaningfully, "Sometimes I reckon she thinks he is. I love her dearly, mind, but she's not right in the head, not now." She waved a hand, dripping water over the floor. "What with the baby, and the shock and everything. But she's not *dangerous*," she added quickly. "I don't mean that. Just. . ."

"Sad."

"Exactly."

"So . . . they didn't give her any evacuees to look after because they thought she wouldn't cope?" Molly glanced round at Rose, and saw that Rose looked anxious too. Perhaps they would have to leave after all, leave this beautiful house, and the bedroom they shared with the striped wallpaper and the flowered curtains – the same print as Rose's new dress. *We should have known it was too perfect to be true*, Molly thought, feeling a hot prickling at the backs of her eyes. It was so hard to think of setting off walking again, even after just two days of being clean and comfortable and cared for.

"Yeah, but they were wrong, weren't they? Cheer up, lovey." Phyllis smiled at her. "You three have been a tonic, you really have. Fussing over you, she's better than I've seen her since she had the news. And you'll be able to help her out with the baby, won't you, big girls like you."

Molly wrinkled her nose a little, but she ducked away so that Phyllis couldn't see. She didn't particularly want to be the sort of big girl who helped look after babies. And she didn't see why John couldn't look after a baby too, actually. But they were unbelievably lucky, she reminded herself, they would do anything, anything they were asked.

"Though you'll be at school soon, of course," Phyllis went on. "Taking you down there on Monday, I heard."

Molly sighed. However much Mrs Tolley was grieving, she was determined to take the very best care of her evacuees. The teacher from the village school walked past the house on her way in the mornings, apparently, and Mrs Tolley had chased her down the lane the day after they arrived and told her that there would be three new pupils. It would be so odd to go back to school without Jean and Sally. She had seen the village school too – it was tiny, nothing like Hanley Road. The headmaster had been in the Territorials, and had been called up, so now there would only be one class, with everyone in together, even though the village's scattering of evacuees had made the school bigger. Mrs Tolley had told them that there was talk of splitting the school into morning and afternoon sessions so that Miss Carey could cope, but it hadn't been popular in the village.

Rose put down her tea towel and wrapped her arms around Molly's waist. She still wasn't talking, but she seemed so much happier – most of the time. There were still moments where she disappeared into herself, and Molly wondered if she was thinking of her grandma. John didn't seem to miss her quite as much, but from what he'd said, Molly thought Rose and her gran had been very close.

"It'll be all right," she whispered now.

"Course it will," said Phyllis brightly. "You'll have my sister Pammie there. She'll look after you."

Molly was trying to be cheerful for Rose's sake, but she wasn't sure how Rose was going to do at school. She was so little. Her first experience of school had been when she and John were staying with the Kemps, and it clearly hadn't gone well, with Nora and Ellen encouraging the others to pick on her. Molly suspected the bullying she'd had at the school had helped stop her talking. Why would she talk, if she was shoved and pinched and laughed at every time she opened her mouth?

"We all will," she told Rose, pressing her hands over Rose's tiny ones on the front of her dress. "You might even like it."

Staring back at the sea of faces in front of her on Monday morning, Molly was terrified, so she couldn't imagine how Rose felt. Rose was clinging on to her hand so tightly that Molly's fingers were aching.

"The Grant children have come from London." Molly twitched. She still wasn't used to their new name – they'd had to pick one that would do for all of them. She didn't even know what John and Rose's real surname was, nor they hers. "It's very nice to have you," Miss Carey was saying. "Now, since we've grown so much with our evacuees, we're a little short on space, so for the moment, John, could you sit there with Michael. And Molly and Rose, you can share this desk with Pammie."

Pammie – that was Phyllis's sister. She looked quite like Phyllis, with dark wavy hair and very pink cheeks. She was waving at them, beckoning them over, and the girls scuttled to sit next to her. Molly crammed Rose in the middle – the desk had a fitted bench that was meant for two; if Rose had been on the outside she'd probably have fallen off.

"My sister told me to look out for you," Pammie whispered. "Which one is it that doesn't talk?"

Molly pointed at Rose, and Rose stared at the names scratched into the top of the desk.

"She'll fit in with Mad Mrs Tolley, then, won't she?" Pammie grinned, and Molly felt her hands grow cold. Pammie might look like Phyllis, but perhaps she didn't share her sister's easy-going sweetness.

216

"She's not mad," she whispered back furiously. "Neither of them are."

"Keep your hair on. Your little sister doesn't talk, and Mrs Tolley's pretending her husband's still alive. She goes to the post office to ask why his letters don't come, did you know that? She's lost it."

"Shut up." Molly stared straight ahead, her eyes glittering with furious tears. But all through the morning, Pammie kept on whispering, sly little digs whenever Miss Carey wasn't watching.

When Miss Carey sent them outside for morning break, Molly lingered in the classroom, with Rose pressed close beside her. Miss Carey turned round from cleaning the board and smiled at them. "Go on outside, girls, get some fresh air. Your brother's disappeared already, hasn't he? Never mind, Pammie will look after you. Won't you, Pammie?"

Molly glanced round to see Pammie waiting by the door, looking angelic and helpful. "Yes, Miss Carey," she murmured, ducking her head and smirking at Molly.

Molly felt Rose's cold fingers creep into hers, and an iron determination grew inside her. No one was going to be cruel to Rose here, whatever it took. She would fight if she had to. She hadn't fought people at Hanley Road, but she'd seen girls do it, rolling over and over and scratching. She could do that. After all, she was Rose's sister now.

"Don't worry," she whispered to the top of Rose's head as they followed Pammie out. "She's not going to do anything to you. Not a single thing."

Pammie seemed to be the queen of the little school. As she led them out on to the patch of grass that surrounded the school, all the other girls hurried to join her, as if she'd summoned them. She was one of the oldest girls, Molly reckoned, but that wasn't what brought them running. Clearly, Pammie said who was who in Marsh End School. Some of these girls gathered round her now were evacuees from London, as she and Rose were; Molly had spotted them from their accents when they spoke up in class. But even though they were strangers, they had clearly accepted Pammie as the leader of all the girls.

"So. . ." Pammie folded her arms and smiled round at her little court. "What's wrong with your sister then? Why doesn't she talk? Miss is going to make her, you know. She'll have all sorts of plans. They won't let her get away with it for long."

"Rose'll talk when she's ready," Molly said, wrapping an arm round Rose's shoulders.

"But *why* doesn't she talk?" another of the girls asked, with a tiny sideways flick of a look at Pammie, to make sure this was allowed.

Molly was silent for a moment. She had known this was coming, she had lain in bed that morning thinking about it, with Rose snuggled in next to her. Rose had grown used to sleeping curled together while they were walking, and even though she had her own beautiful little bed, which she loved, she didn't stay in it for long. Molly had stared at the ceiling, wondering how much to tell. They were supposed to have come straight from their home in London, so only half the truth was possible. They'd told Mrs Tolley that Rose didn't speak because she was missing her gran so much, and that had become part of their accepted story now. Their gran was Mrs Tolley's aunt, everyone thought. It was terribly sad, but almost a mercy for the poor lady, Phyllis had said, given how things were.

But even though grief was a reason, it wasn't going to stop questions. It was unusual for a child to miss a grandparent so dramatically. Molly had worried it over, but she hadn't been able to come up with an answer. In the end she came round to hoping that Rose would be a nine days' wonder, and then perhaps everyone would just get used to her, and leave them alone.

Pammie wasn't going to let that happen.

Molly glanced around for John, but he was off with a group of boys, admiring what looked like a model aeroplane.

"She's wrong in the head," one of the girls

muttered, and all of them stared at Rose. Molly couldn't tell if they pitied her, or they were just frightened.

"Rose does talk sometimes," she claimed.

"No, she doesn't!" Pammie rolled her eyes. "My sister told me. Rose is as silent as the grave, she said."

Molly stared at her, the strange phrase catching in her head. She thought of those cardboard coffins again, and how much they'd frightened her. Frightened was *better*. She'd quite like Pammie to be frightened of her, and Rose. No one wanted to be pitied. She squeezed Rose's hand gently, to tell her it was all right. "She . . . she doesn't talk to anyone here. Not in this world. Because she talks to people beyond the grave."

There was a moment of silence, and then one of the smaller girls spoke up. "You mean, ghosts?"

Molly nodded. One of their neighbours back home gave readings, where she talked to spirits. Her mum didn't approve, but it was important to keep on good terms with the neighbours, so she nodded and smiled to Mrs Petrie, and stopped to speak to her in the street. Molly thought she was fascinating. She had watched people – almost all of them women – walking up to Mrs Petrie's door and glancing around as if they didn't want to be seen. She longed to slip inside that door too, but Mrs Petrie charged a whole five shillings a reading.

"Spirits," she said, so quietly that they all had to lean towards her to hear. "Rose hears the voices of the dead. She can answer them too."

"Did the dead take away her voice?" the small girl asked, gazing round-eyed at Rose.

"Don't be stupid, Eileen!" Pammie broke in. "It's not true. She's just making it up to scare you."

"But Rose *doesn't* talk, Pammie," one of the others pointed out.

"That's because she's round the bend! It's nothing to do with ghosts!"

Molly shrugged. "I can't make you believe me. But I'd be careful."

"What do you mean?" Pammie snapped.

"Just that. Be careful, that's all." Molly gazed at her steadily, and to her surprise, Pammie actually took a tiny step back.

"Are you threatening me?"

"No." Molly heaved a sigh and glanced round the other girls. "I'm just warning you."

They walked home by themselves at the dinner hour, but Mrs Tolley came to meet them at the end of school. She hadn't said that she was going to, and they pulled up short as they saw her waiting with Bertie by the gate into the grassy playground. She must have been worrying about them, Molly realized, feeling rather pleased. It was nice, to have someone fussing. Bertie leaped and barked as he saw them, and Mrs Tolley let him drag her towards them, laughing. "He's missed you this afternoon!" she called.

"What's she doing here?" John muttered. "I was going to see Roy's Meccano. He asked me."

"Well, you can't," Molly murmured back. "It's not polite, not when she's bothered to come and fetch us."

"Just hope she's not planning on doing it every day. Right idiot I'll look. She's waving."

But Molly and Rose had run to meet Mrs Tolley, and Rose was hugging her, carefully round the bulge under her tweed coat. Molly crouched down to hug Bertie, who didn't know whether to wag, or jump up or bark. He huddled next to her, quivering with excitement, and whining softly.

"Silly old thing," John muttered, letting Bertie lick his hands. "What did you do all day without us? Hey?"

"He didn't like it when you went away again after your lunch," Mrs Tolley said, shaking her head. "He followed me round the house looking mournful, and then he sat on my feet when I stopped for a rest this afternoon. He was very good company." She smiled at them. "I came to see if you wanted to go along the street to Aitken's? That's the grocer's, they have some jars of sweets..."

John looked decidedly less grumpy after that. Even without the lure of toffee, or bootlaces, it was interesting to see the shops. They had skirted round the busy main street when they came through the village a few days before. Marsh End was a larger village than most of the ones they'd seen, with proper shops instead of one small one that sold everything, and its own small police station.

"Here for a treat, are we?" The grocer smiled at them over a large grey-brown moustache that made him look as if he'd glued a dead mouse under his nose. Molly tried very hard not to look at it, so she didn't snigger.

The grocer poured them out sweets from the glass jars – treacle toffee for Molly, bullseyes for John, and a sugar mouse with a string tail for Rose. Mrs Tolley paid, and they were just turning to leave when the mouse-moustache man called after them. "Don't forget to register them, Mrs Tolley, will you? For the ration books. Any day now they're saying. Butter and bacon to start with.

You're registered with me, of course, but I don't have these young 'uns."

"Oh. . ." Mrs Tolley nodded. "Oh yes. I hadn't thought, Mr Aitken. Ration books. Of course."

"We don't have ration books," John hissed when they'd untied Bertie and got clear of the shop. "Mr Kemp had that form, a lady came and gave it to him. He went on and on about it. Perhaps he's got our ration books? What are we going to do?"

"What form? What are ration books?" Molly asked worriedly.

"Keep calm," Mrs Tolley murmured, though she didn't sound very calm herself. Rose stopped skipping, and came back to peer at her worriedly. "Oh, I should have thought of this! The form, Molly, the National Register! They came round and counted everyone, on the twenty-ninth of September. That was so they could send out the ration books. They say rationing will start soon. You have to tear little squares out of the book – it's all going to be terribly complicated, I think."

226

She looked at the three of them. "None of you have identity cards? I suppose not... You were out there on your own even back then? I – I thought only a few days... Oh dear." She pressed her hand to her mouth for a moment, and then smiled at the children, showing too many teeth. "Heartburn, that's all. The baby being unhelpful again, little wretch."

"Are they going to find us?" John growled.

"No." Mrs Tolley shook her head firmly. "No, of course not. I don't deny it's tricky, but I'll go to the Food Office in Tadworth tomorrow while you're at school. I shall tell them that you were evacuated, and your mother's been very ill, and somehow you don't have identity cards. They can sort it out, I'm sure. They'll tell me where to go for the identity cards. My poor imaginary cousin Enid, I'm starting to feel quite guilty, saying all this about her."

That night, Rose crept into bed beside her again, and Molly half woke. Rose's feet were cold.

"Don't put your feet on mine! Uuugh, Rose. . ." She shivered and pulled the blankets closer around both of them. It was the first time they'd found to talk alone since she confronted Pammie and the others. There had always been someone else around, John or Mrs Tolley. Molly hadn't told John what she'd done. She'd probably have to, soon, she reckoned. But she wasn't sure what he was going to say, so she reckoned they'd wait and see a little while. See if it worked.

"Did you understand what I said to Pammie?" she whispered in Rose's ear. She smelled of Auntie Lucy's talcum powder.

Rose didn't say anything, of course. But she was perfectly capable of making her feelings known without talking. She snuggled closer against Molly, and then pressed her cold feet against Molly's legs and giggled.

"You didn't mind? I thought it would stop them teasing you. I suppose it might make things worse, though, I don't know." Lying here in the dark it seemed a strange, almost dangerous thing to have done. Molly couldn't help remembering the faces of all those women who went to Mrs Petrie's – their faces when they came out again. pale and tearful and sometimes uplifted.

What had she started?

Chapter Eleven

It only took a couple of days for the gossip about Rose to get back to John. Molly still hadn't told him what she'd done, she'd been putting off doing it, and he glared at her as they came out of school and set out through the village to the house.

"What did you tell all those girls?" he hissed, once they were well away from the others. "Rob asked me whether my little sister had ever shown me a ghost. He was serious! He said he reckoned he'd seen one at the top of his gran's stairs. I hadn't got a clue what he was on about."

Molly wheeled round and shoved him, hard, in the chest. "I had to do something! Pammie was picking on her on the very first day! You weren't anywhere to be seen, were you? Did you want me to let her make Rose's life a misery? Because she would have done."

"Hey!" John protested, but only feebly. "You could have said. I'd have helped."

"I couldn't say, because you were off somewhere with Rob and Michael and Alan Ferris like you always are," Molly pointed out bitterly. "Talking about how to spot a Nazi spy, or whatever. You weren't even thinking about Rose, so I had to do it. And now no one picks on her. Or me," she added as an afterthought.

It was entirely true. Rose had a little china doll as well as her toy cat Samuel now. Eileen had brought it into school on their second day, and pressed it into Rose's hand as they all gathered to march into the classroom. The doll was a nice one, dressed in a tiny scrap of creamy lace, with white socks and little black ankle strap shoes painted on. The shoes still shone, it was that new. "Can she ask them to look out for my brother?" Eileen asked Molly earnestly. "He's gone to be a ship's boy in the navy."

"I – I don't know if it works that way," Molly had murmured. She didn't want to raise Eileen's hopes. She was kind, and she didn't seem to be as worried about Pammie as most of the girls.

"It's all right. Please can she just try? Please, Rose?"

Rose had tucked the doll into her coat pocket and smiled at Eileen, a wide, gap-toothed smile, and nodded.

That had only been the first of the gifts. A tiny bunch of Christmas roses, to intercede for Moira's sick auntie. A packet of mint humbugs, for Annabel's cousin who was in a sanatorium.

No one seemed to have worked out that Rose couldn't tell them what the spirits had actually *said*. Even Pammie seemed to be keeping a truce.

She'd moved along the bench of their desk now, so that she was perching on the very end. It meant that she wasn't touching Rose at all, not even their skirts touching, and it made Molly smile to herself every time she noticed it.

Pammie had been right – Miss Carey *was* trying to convince Rose to talk. But so far her methods were rather feeble. She had kept Rose behind after school to try and bribe her with toffees – that she could have the toffee if she'd only ask for it – and she had looked quite guilty when Molly walked back in from the cloakroom and told her that they needed to go.

"No one knows why Rose isn't talking," Molly told her, trying to be polite even though she didn't feel it.

"I'm sure she could if she only tried," Miss Carey explained, looking a little flustered.

"I don't think Auntie Lucy would want you to push her, miss." If Miss Carey's methods worked and Rose began to speak, the girls would know that they'd been lying. Molly swallowed the hard lump that seemed to have risen in her throat. Did that mean that Rose would have to be silent for ever?

Molly worried over it for days, so much that she kept waking up in the middle of the night, or early in the morning, and then she couldn't get back to sleep. There didn't seem to be any good way to get them out of the deception. If Rose did start talking again, perhaps they could tell it as some sort of miracle? Pammie had started to ask difficult questions again. It was as if she could smell fear, Molly thought wearily as she stared out of their bedroom window. There wasn't actually a lot of point in looking out, it was November now, and black dark at five in the morning. But she was sick of lying in bed with Rose breathing so peacefully next to her. It only made her feel worse, and then she found herself wanting to pinch Rose, so it was better to get up.

The problem was that Pammie was actually right – they couldn't prove that Rose could speak to the spirit world, because of course she didn't. Molly pulled the knitted shawl she was wearing over her nightdress tighter – it was getting so much colder now – and rested her chin on her hands, peering gloomily at the road. Her eyes were adjusting to the darkness now. She might see a fox. But not a wolf. She wrinkled her nose, remembering how hard John had laughed when she'd confessed her fear of wolves out in the country. How was she to know there hadn't been wolves in England for hundreds of years? She didn't think it was all that funny.

She was almost asleep at the windowsill when a faint scuffling sound brought her up with a start. It wasn't a fox – or a wolf – there was a white figure walking down the lane towards the house. A faint, shadowy, white figure that was getting *closer and closer*.

Molly had been spinning ghost stories in the dinner hour for weeks now. John had helped her come up with them, once he'd realized just how well Molly's plan was working to protect Rose.

Working together, their stories had got more and more frightening, so that even though Molly knew that they were all made up, they made her shiver. It was a strange, exciting sort of fear, and she loved the way the girls all listened, clinging on to each other's hands and squeaking, and every so often looking admiringly at Rose, who of course was supposed to be the one who'd told the tales to Molly.

In the middle of the first story, which was about a small girl who had drowned in a well, and walked through the village dripping wet, Mavis had asked how Rose had told Molly all this when she didn't talk. Molly had been frozen for a moment, mouth fishily open. But luckily Eileen had rounded on Mavis and told her not to be so difficult.

"They're sisters! Of course Molly knows too! Did she tell you in a dream, Molly?"

Molly had nodded slowly. "Not quite a dream. More – more a waking dream, I suppose. She just *looks* at me, and I know."

The audience had nodded, and shuddered deliciously, and told Mavis to shush. And that was that.

That first dripping child came back to Molly now as she watched the white figure flap and flutter past the bushes. It was almost at the start of the wall that belonged to the house. Molly wanted to run and hide under her bedcovers, but she couldn't move. Perhaps it was coming for her because she'd lied! It was coming for her, and for Rose!

She gripped the edge of the windowsill so tight that she was sure her fingers must be biting deep wells into the wood. Should she wake Rose and run? Her feet felt leaden, and she was so cold, all over.

Then the ghost tripped over something on the uneven surface of the lane, and swore.

It was like a veil lifting. All at once, Molly could see that the ghost was Alf, the boy who worked in the baker's overnight getting all the bread ready for the morning. He lived with his mum in a tiny cottage further up the lane past the house. He'd have just finished his shift, and he was on his way home to sleep, all whitened and covered with flour. He had an old flour sack wrapped round his shoulders too, to keep him warm on the walk.

Molly pressed her hand over her mouth, trying to stop the rising wave that wanted to wash over her. If she laughed out loud she'd wake Rose. She leaned weakly against the windowsill, her stomach muscles aching with the effort of silent laughter.

Now – that would be a way to shut Pammie up, wouldn't it? Why not show her a real ghost?

"We're going to be in such trouble," Mavis twittered excitedly. "What if my mum wakes up? Oh, I just know she's going to wake up. My sisters would tell on me as soon as they'd spit, I promise you. We're going to be in such trouble. . ."

"Ssshhh, Mavis! You only live two cottages down from the churchyard, you can be home in half a minute!" Pammie hissed. "If your mum misses you, just tell her you ate something funny and you had to go to the outhouse. Anyhow, we won't be out here long. Nothing's going to happen."

"Pammie!" Eileen lifted up the candle lantern to look at her properly. "You mustn't say that. Have some respect!"

"It isn't respectful being out in the churchyard in the middle of the night! We're sitting on a gravestone!" Pammie glanced round at the broken stone box they were all perched on. It was one of the older tombs, and the letters on the inscription were so worn away they were impossible to read. There was only the faintest outline of what might be a carved dove on the headstone.

"Are you scared?" Molly asked. "You can go home, if you like. You're the one who keeps saying me and Rose are making it up. We're only doing this for you."

Rose held Bertie tighter and nodded at Pammie.

"Why would I be scared when nothing's going

to happen?" Pammie repeated. "You're just going to sit here and tell us spooky stories until we start imagining we've seen a ghost. Or maybe you've got your brother to dress up in a sheet. Yeah, like we're stupid enough to fall for that." But her voice wasn't quite steady, and Molly thought the dark was getting to her.

It *was* eerie, being out in the churchyard, with the trees rustling in the wind. The darker pools of shadow behind the stone tombs that stood close to the church door seemed to keep changing shape. Molly was fairly sure that was to do with the clouds being blown across the moonlight, but it still made her heart jump.

"Rose, is there anyone. . . here?" she asked solemnly.

Rose nodded. She let go of Bertie to wave a hand at the worn headstone behind them, and all four girls turned to look.

"You mean – the one we're sitting on?" Eileen asked, her eyes showing white around the edges in the candlelight. "Oh, Rose! Did it – did it come *through* us?"

Rose lifted both hands and shook her head. "She doesn't know," Molly said quickly. "The spirits have ways. Rose says this spirit is old, and it's at peace. It doesn't want anything from us. But it's going to lead us to someone that does. Look, follow Rose. She can see it."

"Lead us where?" Pammie growled as Molly and Rose stood up, and Rose set off slowly along the path round the side of the church, her hands stretched out in front of her in the deep dark. "I'm telling you, Molly Grant, if this is your brother in a sheet..."

"Pammie, shut up." Mavis whispered. "Just shut up."

"Don't you tell me—"

"Shut up and look!"

Pammie turned to look where Mavis was pointing, and saw what had transfixed her and Eileen. A thin, ragged thing, floating above the ground over the churchyard wall. It swirled and gestured, but most of all, it *glowed*.

It was most certainly not John Grant dressed up in a sheet. Bertie, sensing the fear rising from the children, started to growl on a deep, frightening note.

"Pammie. . ." Molly turned to her, looking worried. "Pammie, do you know it?"

"What?" Pammie squeaked.

"Do you know it? Rose says it's asking for you."

"No, it isn't!"

"It is, Pammie, I promise. It's saying you're little Pamela. It knows you." The ghost ran from side to side, as though it was getting increasingly desperate. "I think it wants you to come," Molly said, holding out her hand to Pammie.

"Pammie, that's where your mum's family's plot is, over there by the wall," Mavis whispered. "I've seen you put violets there with your mum. Your great-grandma, she's buried there."

"No, no, no. . ." Pammie gasped, backing away along the path.

"It *is* a woman," Molly agreed, looking at the

ghost with a professional eye, and then at Pammie, stumbling backwards. "You can tell from the shape, she's got a sort of long dress on, hasn't she? Is she saying anything else, Rose?"

"What does she want?" Pammie whimpered.

Molly looked questioningly at Rose for a moment, and then nodded. "She just wants to hold you, Pammie. She says she never got to hold you."

Pammie turned then, running as fast as she could through the churchyard and practically bouncing off the gate on her way out. She was closely followed by Eileen and Mavis, both weeping with fear.

Rose and Molly, left alone in the churchyard, stared at each other, wide-eyed. Then Molly lifted her lantern, and they saw John come creeping out from behind the yew tree. The one he'd climbed to get to the wall, so he could fix the wire that the ghost was hanging from.

"It worked!" He put his arm round Molly's shoulders and gave her the briefest sort of hug – the first time he'd done that, she realized, blinking. "It ran along the wire perfectly. I can't believe they fell for it."

"I nearly fell for it, and I knew it was only that special paint for the blackout," Molly said, shaking her head. "It was terrifying, it looked so real."

"Good thing that Pammie and Phyllis's mum's family isn't buried out in the middle of the churchyard," John said as he started to climb back up the yew tree to claw down the end of the wire. "We couldn't have made it look so real if we were just waving it about on the end of a mop or something. Why did Pammie get so upset when you said the ghost wanted to hold her?"

Molly grinned. "Phyllis told me. She was telling me about how her mum's family all live till they're really old – their great-grandma died the day before Pammie was born. So she never got to hold Pammie, and it was ever so sad."

John unhooked the other end of the horizontal wire and dropped the bundle of phosphorescent rags down to Molly and Rose.

"We'd better get home. We've been out ages, and we've still got to bury this."

"Bury it?" Molly stared at him. "Why? It's not as if it's actually Pammie's great-grandma."

"You want Phyllis finding it when she comes to clean tomorrow? She's not stupid, Molly. If Pammie tells anyone she saw a ghost, Phyllis is going to put two and two together." John jumped down beside her, staggering a little. His cut leg still wasn't quite healed, but he'd insisted on being part of the ghost – Molly had made him feel guilty, telling him he wasn't sticking up for his little sister.

"Maybe. But I reckon Pammie won't tell. She'll be too embarrassed that she ran home."

"Eileen and Mavis will though. You wait. It'll be round the village by the time half the school's gone home to dinner and back again."

Chapter Twelve

"Never thought I'd actually be sick of snow," John growled.

Back in London, snow hadn't been like this. It was dirty in minutes, the cars and carts and vans churning it up to muddy slush. And it never lasted this long. After two months of snow, everyone had built all the snowmen and snow hides and snow houses they could want. Snowball fights weren't funny any more, particularly when Martin Egham decided to put a stone in a snowball and left Roy bleeding from a cut face. The reddish hole where the blood had melted in had been there for days, until the next fall.

Towards the end of January, an ice storm swirled in, collapsing the telegraph wires and leaving the village stranded. Mrs Tolley was getting bigger and bigger, and Molly was terrified by the huge drifts that kept blowing up against the doors. The lane was practically up to her waist, and no one had been down it in anything but a sledge for days. What if the baby started to come, and no one could reach them?

Molly and John and Rose had to help more with the housework, and the cooking, which was more complicated since the rationing had started at last. Only on butter and bacon and ham, as Mr Aitken had said, but the butter ration seemed to go hardly anywhere, and sandwiches these days had only the slimmest possible wafer of ham. All three of them had ration books now, and identity cards, although Mrs Tolley had come home from the Food Office seething about the officious way she'd been made to wait and queue, and wait some more, and then sent off to a completely different office a bus ride away, to be told that she hadn't been given the right forms in the first place.

But they belonged now. The house was their official address on the little buff-coloured cards, neatly inked in.

Apart from the cards, and the rationing, the war seemed to have stalled – the snow had stopped everything, Molly thought. There was no school either, since the little building just couldn't be kept warm enough.

Auntie Lucy found as many of her old books as she could, and they had Snakes and Ladders, Molly's Christmas present, and a set of lead soldiers that John had been given, with a little round hut that was a gun emplacement on the Maginot Line, and an anti-aircraft gun to fire. Auntie Lucy had sent away to London for the presents, except for Rose's, which was a little dolls' house made out of an orange crate, and furnished with scraps of fabric, and beds made of matchboxes. Rose spent hours lying in front of it, endlessly arranging and rearranging her cat and her doll in and out of the tiny rooms.

Snakes and Ladders was a very good game, but only if there were other people who wanted to play it too. John was too busy tracking possible Nazi parachutists through the snow with Roy and the others; he'd even taken Bertie as a bloodhound. Molly had pointed out that Bertie was bored with snow too, but John had insisted. She expected that when they came back, John would be carrying him. Rose was no good, she only wanted to play dolls.

Molly had struggled down the lane earlier on to find one of the girls from school, but after she'd made the effort to get all the way into the village to be told that Eileen had a septic cold and wasn't allowed out, she gave up and stayed indoors. Lumping around the house wishing for someone her own age – or at least close – she remembered

Vicky's label, still tucked in the lining of her suitcase. She had promised that she'd write, but she had forgotten all about it.

Dear Vicky,

Do you remember me? I met you on the train when your school was being evacuated. You and your sister and your friends tried to help me hide my dog, Bertie.

I got off the train at – actually I still don't know where it was, since the sign was painted out. Bertie and I are living with a lady I call Auntie Lucy, and two other children who had run away as well. It wasn't because of having a dog, they had been evacuated and the people looking after them were very cruel.

Is the house where your school is nice? Did you find a secret passage? Did Sarah make it up with Gwen or did the other girl (I've forgotten her name) make Gwen not like her any more?

Please write back, we are snowed in and everything is deadly dull.

With love and kisses,
Molly

She hesitated about sending it. If she wanted an answer, she would have to put the Brook Lodge address, and then Vicky might decide to tell Miss Reynolds where Molly was. Molly didn't think she would, but really, how could she tell? She'd only known Vicky a few hours. Vicky's parting order to write had kept coming back to her, though. While she and Bertie and the others had been walking she couldn't, of course. Now she didn't have an excuse.

She *wanted* to send the letter, she realized. She wanted to feel connected to someone, somewhere. She had been worrying on and off about her mother and Stella. Did they miss her? Were they still looking for her? How had she made them feel, by disappearing? Molly was still sure that she had been right to run away – but she wished she hadn't had to. She had seen how much Rose missed her grandma, and how broken Mrs Tolley was by the loss of her husband. Mum and Stella didn't know where she was; they didn't know if she were alive or dead. She had done that.

She couldn't write to Mum. Even if she didn't put the address on, there would still be the postmark. Mum would take the letter straight to the police (the police must be looking for her – the thought made Molly squirm) and they would know where to start looking. The only way she could post a letter would be to send it from somewhere else, and she wasn't going anywhere, no one was. Even letters were taking days and days, because of the snow. Trains were arriving days late, it was that bad, Phyllis had said.

Molly looked down at the letter to Vicky, starting

to smile. Vicky – Vicky could send her letter. Then it would be postmarked from somewhere in Norfolk. She wasn't entirely sure how many miles away Norfolk was, but she knew from the map Miss Carey used for geography lessons that they were in Essex, and there was all of Suffolk in between. Surely that was far enough?

At the bottom of her letter to Vicky, she added a postscript.

PS Please will you post the letter I've enclosed for my mum and my sister? I just want them to know that I'm safe. Please please please do not tell them my address! Don't tell anyone. Hide this letter in the secret passage, if you did find one. Love, Molly

Then she took another piece of paper from the little box of writing paper and envelopes on Auntie Lucy's desk in the sitting room, and sat staring at it. How long was it since she had seen her mum and Stella? Molly counted through the months on her fingers, and then leaned back in her chair, the breath stolen out of her. Five months. How could it be that long?

They would think she was dead.

Biting miserably at her lips, Molly started to write.

Dear Mum and Stella,

Please don't worry about me. I heard you talking about Bertie and Tom going to the vet to be put to sleep, so I decided to run away with Bertie. I took Tom too, but he jumped out of the basket on the way. I hope he got home safe. I hope he's still with you.

I am safe and staying with a very nice lady. She is going to have a baby soon, but her husband was killed in an accident and she needs someone to look after her.

Stella, if you're in the ATS now, I

hope you like it.

I'm sorry that I've made you worry about me.

Love, Molly

It was a very bad letter, she decided, reading it back. Miss Carey would have called it poor. It was jerky and sharp and uncomfortable, but that was how she felt. At least they would know that she was safe.

Molly sealed it in an envelope and wrote on the address, and added a stamp – they were in the letter paper box too. She looked round as Auntie Lucy came slowly into the room, wrapped in layers of shawls and scarves.

"Is it all right that I've taken two stamps? I can pay for them, I've still got sixpence left." The rest of her money had gone on buying sweets for Christmas presents.

"You're writing to your mother?" Auntie Lucy asked, holding tight to the back of a chair. She looked stricken. "I – I thought – you want her to come and get you?"

"No!" Molly shook her head, her hair flicking round her face with the force of it. "No, of course not! She might still try to take Bertie. But I haven't seen her or my sister for five months, Auntie Lucy. I just thought that I should. In case they think that I'm. . ." She didn't want to say *dead* to Auntie Lucy, who looked precarious enough hanging on to that chair as it was. Instead she held out the letter. "I'm posting it to Vicky – she's a girl I met on a train, and she gave me her label so I could write to her. The other stamp's on the letter to Mum, inside. If Vicky posts it, it won't be postmarked anywhere near here, do you see?"

"Yes. That's very clever, Molly." Auntie Lucy eased herself down so that she was actually sitting on the chair, and sighed. "I hadn't thought, until now, how much I would miss you three if you went away. Which isn't to say that I don't know you must go home sometime," she added hurriedly. "It's very good that you're writing to your mother." She laid a gloved hand on her stomach. "She must be frantic."

"I suppose," Molly agreed uncomfortably. "But you know why I had to do it. I did have to." She could hear her voice rising to a question.

"Yes. . ."

"I'm not going back," she said again, her eyebrows drawing together in a stubborn glare. "Not till the war's over and it doesn't matter any more."

Auntie Lucy sighed. "I think you'll be here awhile, Moll." She gazed vaguely out of the window at the banked snow, and shivered.

It took so long for a reply to come back from Vicky that Molly gave up dashing home from school at the dinner break to see if there was a letter. By the end of February there was still snow about in patches, tucked in the lee of walls, or behind hedges, but the huge drifts had disappeared, swelling the stream that ran along the side of the lane to a torrent laden with lumps of greyish ice. There began to be primroses in the banks along the stream a few weeks later, and then violets. By the time the lambs started to appear in the fields, there was hardly any snow to be seen at all.

There had been good news from the war in February, when hundreds of British prisoners had been released from the hold of a German supply ship, the Altmark, in Norwegian waters. For weeks everyone had been freeing prisoners in the playground, and shouting joyfully, "The navy's here!"

Molly and John were racing down the lane with Rose clinging on to John's back, rescuing her from the Germans, and almost dropping her into the icy waves (the stream) when Molly suddenly stopped dead. Auntie Lucy was at the door in the wall, leaning sideways, white-faced.

"What's the matter?" Molly asked, starting to run again. "Is it the baby?"

Auntie Lucy nodded, and then closed her eyes, bracing herself against the wall. She seemed to struggle against something inside her – was the baby fighting to come out? – and then she shuddered and sighed. "Yes. I tried to telephone, but I couldn't get through, then I thought you would be coming back soon. Could you get Nurse Morris? Tell her the baby's coming."

John slid Rose down to the ground and began to run back along the lane. Molly wrapped Auntie Lucy's arm around her neck and, with Rose pushing from behind, half dragged her back into the house.

"Could you get up the stairs?" Molly panted, standing in the hallway and looking up. Auntie Lucy moaned, but she took a few steps towards the staircase. It hadn't felt that long when Molly and Rose had raced down it in the morning, but it seemed to take hours to go up it now. When John arrived back with the nurse they were still a few steps from the top, all of them sitting there with Auntie Lucy slumped against the wall, sweaty and pale.

Before they could say anything, Molly and Rose and John found themselves shooed downstairs, with instructions to boil a kettle for tea, and not get in the way.

"We weren't in the way," Molly muttered, banging the kettle on to the gas stove. "If it hadn't been for us, that nurse wouldn't even be here! What happened to the telephone anyway, is the pole down again?"

John shrugged. "Don't know. I wasn't looking, just running. Are we supposed to take that tea upstairs when we've made it?"

"I expect so. It isn't going to do much good down here, is it?"

"You'd better do it then." John blushed scarlet. "In case . . . you know."

Molly smirked at him. His face was really very funny. "You could keep your eyes closed and just hold the cup round the door," she suggested.

They made the nurse several cups of tea, and then more for Dr Simpson when he arrived a few hours later. By then John had almost stopped being embarrassed about the mysterious things happening upstairs. He helped Molly make a rice pudding, since it was the only thing she knew how to cook by herself that they had the ingredients for, and they thought it might be good for Auntie Lucy after the baby was born. Rice pudding was nourishing, John and Rose's gran had always said.

There were quite a lot of noises upstairs – footsteps thudding back and forth, and cries that made Rose creep out to the bottom of the staircase, and then run back in a fright. But no one called them, and they didn't dare go up to investigate.

"Everything's ready for this baby, isn't it?" John asked, wincing at a muffled groaning noise from above them. "I mean, there's nothing we need to do."

Molly shook her head. "She's got boxes and boxes of stuff. Her mother keeps knitting things, and her sister. That's what's in those parcels. There's a cradle all ready, it's in Auntie Lucy's room."

John frowned. "Do you think they'll come and visit? Auntie Lucy's mum and her sister."

Molly looked thoughtful. "Maybe. Her mother's

not well though, she's got arthritis and doesn't go out much. And her sister's got three children. We might be all right."

John sighed. "That's not good enough, Molly. What if they do come and Phyllis or someone from the village mentions that we're Cousin Enid's children? We're sunk."

Molly sighed. "I know, I thought of that too. Perhaps we could say they were mixed up, and our mother is Peter's cousin, not Auntie Lucy's? She could still have called her a cousin, couldn't she? And both Peter's parents died a few years back, she told me, so they aren't going to turn up."

All the same, the warm, pretty kitchen felt less safe and certain than it had a few moments before. *We've got identity cards,* Molly told herself. *We look like we belong, even if it is all a lie.* Every so often she wondered what *would* happen when the war was over – how would she go from Molly Grant back to Molly Mason?

Did she even want to?

Stella wouldn't be back at home, Molly was almost sure. She had seen a feature about ATS girls in Phyllis's picture paper. The uniform looked dowdy – the skirts were too long, and the jackets were shapeless, Molly thought – but one of the girls was riding a motorbike, with breeches and boots on, and there were two others in overalls, leaning against an anti-aircraft gun as if they owned it.

Stella was one of those girls now. She had signed up. Whatever happened – even if her little sister had disappeared, and no one knew where she was, and she might be dead – she had left home. She'd taken her chance and got out of Mum's grip, just as Molly had. If Stella was riding round London on a motorbike, she was never going to go back when the war was over. It would be just Molly and Mum. Molly would be shut up in the shop whenever she wasn't at school. She wouldn't even be able to go to the park with her friends without being grilled when she got home about where she'd been. It wouldn't be like Marsh End, where she could go out wandering with Rose and John, or picking primroses with Eileen. Sometimes they'd even taken a sandwich with them, and been out for hours. No one minded. No one made her feel guilty.

There was a creak of floorboards behind them in the passage, and Molly jumped up. Dr Simpson was putting his coat back on in the hallway, and he smiled at her. "Give them a while to rest and tidy up before you go and see them."

"Is the baby here?" Molly asked, looking up the stairs eagerly. "Is Auntie Lucy all right? Is it a boy or a girl?"

"Your cousin and the baby are both very well. You should ask her if it's a boy or a girl. Goodnight, all of you." He shrugged into his coat, and nodded to them as he opened the front door.

"It's late," John murmured. "Rose is asleep on the kitchen table. Shall we go and ask if Auntie Lucy wants the rice pudding? Maybe the nurse too?"

"Your cousin wants to see you." Nurse Morris

came down the stairs, looking a little disapproving. "Be quick please, she ought to be resting. Where's the little one?"

"I'll get her. She fell asleep." Molly hurried back to fetch her, but Rose was grizzly and only half awake and had to be coaxed up the stairs.

Auntie Lucy was in bed, with a worryingly small blanket-wrapped bundle on her lap. Molly wasn't sure if she had ever seen a very new baby – she had never realized how little they were. But the nurse seemed to be pleased with it, cluckily encouraging Auntie Lucy to show the little dear off.

Rose drooped between John and Molly, and Auntie Lucy smiled exhaustedly at her. "Take her to bed, Molly, she's too tired to fuss about the baby now. It's a little boy, Rose, you can see him properly tomorrow."

"What's he called?" John asked, and Auntie Lucy's face looked as creased and fragile as the baby's for a moment.

"Peter, I suppose."

Chapter Thirteen

The excitement of the new baby was almost eclipsed for Molly by an answer to her letter at last. A small pale blue envelope arrived one Saturday morning, with Miss M. Grant and the address written on in perfectly neat sloping handwriting. It took her a few seconds to realize what it must be, and then she could hardly tear the envelope open.

The letter started with a scrawled note across the top of the paper, as if it had been written on afterwards.

*

I've been waiting to post this for ages! First there
was all that snow, and then I got bronchitis and
I wasn't allowed outside for weeks and weeks.
You must have given up. Write back soon! (Did
you hear the news about the Altmark? It's so
exciting!) I'll put your letter to your mother in the
postbox too.

Dear Molly,

It's so exciting being part of a secret letter
drop, like something out of a film. I will post the
letter to your mother when I post this one, but it
won't be until tomorrow, and only then if we're
allowed out. It keeps snowing and Miss Hilton
is so strict, it feels like we've been shut up inside
for months.

Auntie Lucy isn't your real aunt? Who is
she? Are you absolutely sure that the other two
children aren't spies or fifth columnists? You
have to be careful about these things, and I
must say it all sounds awfully suspishous and

quite exciting.

Sarah had an absolutely enormous bust-up with Gwen, and it was all Meg's fault, she's very mean (so is Sarah though sometimes). Sarah sulked for weeks, but she's palled up with Monica now so it's all right.

Please write back and tell me that you're not being captured by Germans.

Yours very sinserely,

Vicky

It was the first letter Molly had ever had all of her own, and it felt so precious. Vicky was right – she had given up. She'd wondered if perhaps the school had moved, or Vicky had just not cared enough to write. They had only known each other an hour or two, after all, and half that time they'd been asleep. Perhaps those posh girls hadn't wanted to be bothered. . .

But now she read it over and over, giggling at the thought of Sarah fighting with those others, and teachers fussing about snow and cold. She wasn't entirely sure what fifth columnists were – some sort of spy? She would have to ask John, he seemed to know everything about spies and Germans and saboteurs.

She had better write back at once, she decided. She could reassure Vicky that John and Rose most definitely weren't spies, and tell her all about Pammie, and their cleverness with the ghost.

The freeing of the prisoners from the *Altmark* seemed to be the last good news for a while. The prime minister gave a speech in April saying that Hitler had missed the bus, and as if he had been listening, the Germans invaded Denmark and Norway three days later. The Allied troops sent to counterattack lasted six weeks, and then had to retreat as the German forces stormed their way across Europe. At the beginning of May they attacked Holland and Belgium, and anyone could see how close that was to France. Miss Carey was beginning to look as though she regretted the maps pinned up around the classroom.

Chamberlain resigned as prime minister, and was replaced by Churchill, who at least talked a good war. But the German tanks were grinding through Luxembourg to France. The queen of the Netherlands went into exile in England as Holland fell, and then Belgium. John's toy Maginot Line fortress was out on the floor of his little room, with the anti-aircraft gun polished shiny next to it, but the real version hadn't held the Germans back. By mid-May, they were pouring into France, Maginot Line or not, and the British forces fighting with the French were pressed further and further back towards the coast.

The troops were rescued from Dunkirk, but the stirring story of the Little Ships that struggled out to carry the soldiers home was the story of a retreat, however gallant it sounded. The BEF were back home, but they were broken.

Molly and John and Rose had been home from

school for dinner, as they always were. Auntie Lucy had cooked a vegetable pie, from a recipe she'd heard on the wireless. Meat was rationed now, and seemed to be harder and harder to get hold of. It was mostly carrot and a bit of cheese, and not very interesting, but after all those weeks of biscuits and stolen apples, no one complained. They left Auntie Lucy listening to the wireless and washing up while Peter slept in a basket on the kitchen table.

They were a little way down the lane when Rose pulled suddenly at John's sleeve, her face panicked.

"What?" John shook her off. "Come on, we'll be late back."

Rose shook her head stubbornly and turned back towards the house.

"Rose, we don't have time," Molly called, but Rose stopped, digging her hand into the little pocket on the cardigan Auntie Lucy had knitted her. It came out empty.

Molly sighed. "She's left that cat," she told John. "Look, that's what she's saying. We'll have to go back and get it, you know what she's like about Samuel."

Samuel was still Rose's most precious thing, loved even more than the china doll from Eileen, even though he was faded, and he'd lost one of his green bead eyes. Auntie Lucy had sewn a new bead on, but it wasn't the same green, and Samuel looked cross-eyed now.

"Oh, all right then. But we'd better run!" John grabbed Rose's hand and hauled her on down the lane, racing her along so that they burst through the back door and almost fell into the scullery, Bertie bouncing around their feet and whining delightedly. He shot out of the door to nuzzle at Molly, excited to see her again when he'd resigned himself to a lonely afternoon. She was too busy fussing over him to notice the strange silence for a moment. Then all at once she pushed Bertie down, and hurried after John and Rose into the kitchen. Something was wrong – she could feel it. They were standing across the table from Auntie Lucy, all of them frozen staring at each other.

On the table, next to Peter in his basket, was a gun.

"What's that for?" John asked huskily as Molly pulled Rose back against the door to the scullery. Phyllis's words were ringing in her head. Auntie Lucy wasn't well still – but she wasn't *dangerous*. Molly had seen her exhausted, and sad. She'd seen her crying in the garden in the middle of the night in her slippers. But she'd never been scared. She and John and Rose made Auntie Lucy better, Phyllis had said so.

"What are you doing with it?" John demanded.

Auntie Lucy put down the cloth she was holding and let out a shaky breath. "I was cleaning it. You have to. Guns get – gummed up."

"But why have you *got* a gun?" Molly asked. She knew that some of the men in the village had them for shooting rabbits, but she'd only ever seen a gun at the cinema. She was sure Auntie Lucy didn't go out potting rabbits – she bought them, from the butcher, or Phyllis's brother George.

There was a snuffly wail from the basket, and Auntie Lucy sighed and picked Peter up. She sat down at the table with him, pushing the gun out of the way and draping a muslin over her blouse before she unbuttoned it. "It was on the one o'clock bulletin," she explained as Peter began to suck noisily. John turned sideways. He still went red every time she fed the baby.

"What was?" Molly asked, coming to sit at the table too. Rose perched on her lap, and reached out to tickle Peter's little pink feet.

"France has fallen." Auntie Lucy closed her eyes, but she looked calmer now, as though feeding Peter had settled her back. "Marshal Pétain surrendered. He's asked for an armistice."

John sat down next to Molly, his face going from red to white. "France has gone? It's only us then."

The Germans were ready, just across the sea. There was only a little over twenty miles of water between them.

"Are you going to shoot Germans?" Molly asked, her voice trembling. She couldn't imagine Auntie Lucy guarding them with a gun.

"No." Auntie Lucy stroked Peter's tiny hand, gripping fiercely on to the side of her blouse. "No, the gun wasn't for Germans, Molly. It was for when they come. It was for us."

IF THE GERMANS COME, BY PARACHUTE, AEROPLANE OR SHIP, YOU MUST REMAIN WHERE YOU ARE. THE ORDER IS "STAY PUT".

Molly and John had hidden the gun, and Auntie Lucy hadn't asked them where, even though she must have noticed that it had disappeared off the kitchen table when she came downstairs from changing Peter. But they had gone back to school by then, and no one cared that they were late. Everyone was discussing the news in anxious whispers.

By the time they left school that afternoon, Ted Bottle, the ploughman for Wilson's farm, was up at the top of the road into the village with his team, pulling a huge tree trunk into place. The blacksmith was there ready to fit a wheel on one end, so it could be dragged across the road to block the way.

The leaflet arrived by post a few days later, titled *If the INVADER comes*. They hid it from Auntie Lucy before she could read it, but John seized on the order to *KEEP WATCH*. He had a notebook and pencil in his pocket always, and he borrowed Peter Tolley's birdwatching binoculars and took them up to the attic, where he could climb out on the roof. He stayed up there for hours every day after school, watching for parachutists, sometimes with Martin or Roy for company. It was vital work, he explained to Molly – the Germans were dropping soldiers dressed in blue uniforms the exact colour of the sky, with transparent parachutes. Only the keenest watcher would spot them.

Molly wasn't sure she believed in transparent parachutes. Her mum had never stocked any material that was more see-through than muslin, and that wouldn't be strong enough, though of course the government might have come up with something new. But there were so many stories as the summer wore on and the dogfights began in the sky above them. Apparently Germans were landing all over the place dressed as policemen and nuns and nurses. John was bitterly disappointed that he hadn't seen one, but at least he was an expert on planes. Martin had a plane-spotter manual, and the boys huddled over it in spare moments at school.

The first fight they saw was on a Saturday afternoon, a blissful, quiet sunny day, when they were helping Auntie Lucy with the garden. The vegetable patch they'd seen when they arrived the year before had now been extended to cover most of the space, with little grass paths winding between the beds. Auntie Lucy had taken the wireless broadcasts and posters telling everyone to Dig for Victory to heart. Molly thought that she was desperate to be busy. Besides, small Peter liked to be outdoors, he was always happier sitting on a rug in the garden, sucking on peapods, or trying to catch leaves.

Molly had picked a huge basket of runner beans (which was going to mean beans with everything for ages, sadly) and was having a rest on the rug with the baby, showing him butterflies. The garden was full of the buzzing drone of bumblebees, lumbering around the buddleia bush that grew by the wall. Molly lay back on her elbows, watching them sleepily. They were so loud.

She didn't realize what she was hearing until John came tearing up the garden from the compost heap, screaming something about a Messerschmitt.

Auntie Lucy and Rose appeared from the raspberry canes, and they stood staring upwards, watching the planes streak across the sky.

"That's a Messerschmitt Bf 109E," John gabbled. He was practically jumping up and down. "And those are Spitfires chasing it. I expect it'll go into a dive to escape, they can't turn as well as the Spits, he'll be trying to disengage."

"They're so close." Auntie Lucy shuddered. "I didn't think – that we'd be able to see them. Not like this."

"You can see the swastika on the tail," John shouted over her, not listening. "Look at them, look at them, they're going to get him!"

"There's smoke," Molly said, narrowing her eyes. "Smoke coming out of the tail. I think it's coming down."

Auntie Lucy snatched Peter up, looking around as though she thought they ought to run.

"It isn't going to be anywhere near," John told her, in the voice of an expert. "They're still very high. I should think he'll try and put down in a field somewhere, he's going to manage a controlled landing."

The pilot did land the plane, a few miles away in a field, as John had predicted, but it was only the beginning of a summer of battles across the sky.

"I don't think you should be looking at that." Auntie Lucy tried to tug the newspaper out of Molly's hands, but Molly hung on stubbornly.

"I ought to see it. Mum's there, and maybe Stella too. I don't even know where she is!" Molly slapped the newspaper down on the kitchen table. It was the first picture she had seen of the bomb damage in London. Even though there had been descriptions in the papers before, very few photographs had been published. Molly could see why – the picture was terrifying. It was meant to be funny – or maybe brave, she wasn't quite sure which. The milkman had a white jacket on, and a crate of bottles, just as usual, but he was walking across a heap of rubble and dirt and broken bits of house that stretched back all the way along the street. There was a fountain of smoke or steam rising up behind him, and two firemen in helmets were struggling with a hose. If that milkman had any sense he wouldn't be going anywhere near.

This was why Stella had wanted her out of London.

Molly smoothed the page straight again, trying to work out if the street looked familiar. There was no reason it should be anywhere near the shop, and Mum. The milkman didn't look like their milkman. But that picture of the smiling man in all the wreckage made the solemn reports on the news broadcasts seem so much more real.

"Perhaps you should write to her," Auntie Lucy suggested, sitting down next to Molly. "You could find out how she is. What your sister's doing."

"Not unless I put an address on for a reply, and then she'll know where I am!" Molly protested, looking round at Bertie, curled in his basket in the corner of the kitchen. Peter had shuffled over to the basket on his bottom, and he was reaching for Bertie. Molly jumped up to fetch him, and put him back at the other side of the kitchen. Immediately the baby began to wriggle grimly forward again. He adored Bertie and his main aim in life was to get in the basket with him and suck Bertie's ears. The dog didn't particularly love Peter back, but he put up with being treated as a toy. He was watching Peter over the edge of the basket, as if he was working out how much longer he had to doze in peace.

"Perhaps you should do it anyway."

Molly glared angrily at Auntie Lucy. "I did all of this so that she wouldn't know where we were!" she protested. "I can't let her find us now! That would be – just – *stupid*. And you'd get into trouble! You lied for us to get us our identity cards, you had to swear in front of a magistrate." She looked round at the baby, halfway across the room again. "What about Peter? You're all he's got."

Auntie Lucy nodded. "I know. But look at that photograph, Molly. This isn't right. The world isn't supposed to be like this, with houses blown to bits and children sent away from their parents."

"The street isn't near where I lived," Molly muttered. "I can tell. It's different. Mum's going to be all right, and so's Stella. She's out riding a motorbike, or sending wireless signals. Not at home, anyway."

"All right." Auntie Lucy paused. "Molly. . ."

"What?"

"Talking about your family . . . Phyllis told me something. Her younger sister was talking, and she had some strange story about Rose." Auntie Lucy gave a high, rather unnatural laugh. "Phyllis is terribly superstitious . ." She glanced up at Molly nervously. "She said Rose can talk to the dead. That that's why she doesn't speak out loud."

Molly swallowed hard. It had been so long since she'd made up the story. It was October now. They had lived at Marsh End nearly a year. She had been waiting for Auntie Lucy to hear about Rose's gift, she'd been ready. But it had taken so long, and she'd forgotten what she meant to say. So she only nodded.

"It is just a silly story, isn't it?" Auntie Lucy traced the herringbone pattern on her tweed skirt.

Molly wasn't sure what answer she wanted.

"Rose doesn't talk," she said hesitantly.

"I always thought that was because she was grieving." Auntie Lucy looked up again. "Though I suppose losing her grandmother – perhaps that was the way in? Was that what happened, Molly? She was so distraught that her gran's spirit came back to comfort her? It opened the way for other spirits to speak to Rose too?"

Molly stared back at her, saying nothing. It constantly amazed her how much of this story people wanted to tell for themselves. She almost didn't have to say anything.

"Molly, do you think Rose could speak to Peter for me?"

Molly had known that this was what she was leading up to, of course it was. But it still made her start. She remembered those pale, anxious women tapping on Mrs Petrie's door back home. Molly didn't want Auntie Lucy to be like that, she was meant to be their safe haven, however damaged she might be. She put her hand to her mouth, gnawing on the dry skin around her thumbnail. What was she supposed to do now?

"I only want him to know about small Peter," Auntie Lucy explained, patting at her eyes with a handkerchief. "He was so excited, when he knew that a baby was coming. . ."

Molly nodded. She could see that. It must have been the most awful time to lose her husband, when something so special was about to happen. She wanted to tell Auntie Lucy that he knew, that he was happy, he was watching over them. She had done it for Eileen, and all the others at school. It hadn't really done any harm, had it? Her lies had kept Rose safe, and that had been more important than the truth. Molly was sure about that.

But still. . . This felt different. The expression on Auntie Lucy's face was so hopeful, her eyes wide and bright.

She couldn't do this.

"Perhaps tonight? When I've put Peter to bed?"

Auntie Lucy suggested hopefully. "Would Rose ask him then?"

Molly swallowed hard, certain all at once that she was right. It wouldn't just be her lying, it would be Rose too. They'd have to put on some awful act, pretending to hear voices the way they had in the churchyard. She didn't mind lying to Pammie – in fact, she'd do it again, any day. But not Mrs Tolley. It was funny, really, since a lot of what Auntie Lucy had done to keep them was to tell lie after lie.

"She can't. . ." Molly said, her voice shaking.

Auntie Lucy stared at her, eyes widening with hurt. "But – but why not? Phyllis said she'd done it for the children at school."

"It isn't real," Molly told her huskily. "We made it up. *I* made it up. Phyllis's sister, she's a bully. She was picking on Rose because she doesn't talk. So I said it was because Rose was talking to dead people."

She saw Auntie Lucy flinch at the words, but she

couldn't take them back.

"You were right – you said it was just a silly story." She looked at Auntie Lucy pleadingly. "I never wanted to lie. I – I had to. I couldn't let them hurt Rose again."

Auntie Lucy nodded, but Molly wasn't sure that she'd actually heard. She stood up shakily, and then picked up little Peter, huddling him close just as he was about to reach for Bertie's basket. The baby let out a wail of outrage, but Auntie Lucy didn't whisper to him, or jiggle him on her hip. She just walked out of the kitchen, quite silent, and carried the roaring child up the stairs.

Molly turned wearily as the back door clicked, and John and Rose came in, looking hopeful. "Is supper ready?" John asked.

"No," Molly told him flatly. "I don't know if there is any supper. There's bread in the bread bin."

"What happened?" John frowned at her. "Are you sick? You look odd." Rose came to lean against Molly and stroke her hair.

Molly folded her arms on the table and put her head down on them. "Auntie Lucy wanted Rose to talk to her husband. I had to tell her Rose couldn't, and she was . . . upset." She felt Rose's hands still, and there was a little sigh against her ear.

John said nothing for a moment, then he marched round in front of her and glared. "I knew that was a stupid idea!"

"No, you didn't!" Molly sat up angrily. "You joined in! You helped us make the ghost. You can't just decide it was wrong now."

"I never liked it," he muttered. "I was just sticking up for Rose." He grabbed hold of his little sister, pulling her away from Molly so she stumbled and squeaked. Rose pushed him, but she didn't try to go back to Molly. "Now what's going to happen? What if Auntie Lucy sends us away because you lied?"

"So it's all my fault?" Molly said bitterly. She couldn't tell if he really thought that, or if he just wanted to blame her so he didn't have to blame himself.

John growled something and stamped out of the kitchen. Rose trailed after him, looking back at Molly with worried, lost eyes.

Chapter Fourteen

They didn't see Auntie Lucy again that night. Molly heard Peter wake up sometime much later, and then Auntie Lucy's footsteps as she went to shush him. She sat up in bed, wondering if she should go and tell Auntie Lucy she was so, so sorry. But she wasn't brave enough.

No one woke Molly the next morning. It was a Saturday, so there was no school to hurry for, but it felt odd anyway. She could tell from the light that it was later than she'd usually get up. Any normal day, Rose would have woken her by now, wanting Molly to come downstairs and help her cut bread for breakfast. She was quite capable of cutting it herself, but she liked having Molly to do things for her.

Rose had slept the whole night in her own bed.

Molly got dressed hurriedly, and ran downstairs, desperate to find Auntie Lucy and the others. She had to say something, even though she didn't know what. Even Bertie had deserted her.

When she was at the landing, where the stairs turned, someone knocked loudly on the front door, and Molly jumped back against the wall. Then she shook herself. It was just the post. She sped down the rest of the staircase, and opened the door.

It wasn't the post. Mrs Tennant, the vicar's wife, was standing at the top of the steps with a policeman next to her. Not even the policeman from the village, Martin's dad, but someone Molly had never seen before.

Had someone told on them, for the stunt in the churchyard? After all this time? Molly stood holding the door and staring at them, wondering what to say.

Mrs Tennant smiled at her, but she looked upset. She was one of Auntie Lucy's friends and Molly had seen her before, quite often. She came round to have tea, and always brought something, often a spare egg from her chickens. Mrs Tennant was the one who had made sure that Auntie Lucy didn't get any evacuees, because she was worried about her, and thought she wouldn't cope. She was the billeting officer, the one whose job it was to find foster homes for all the evacuees. . .

Molly held tighter on to the door, looking at the policeman. She was dizzy. Perhaps this was a punishment, for lying about Rose talking to the dead? It was God, or Fate, or just very bad luck.

"Was that someone at the door?" Auntie Lucy was coming in through the kitchen – Molly could hear her rinsing her hands in the scullery, she must have been gardening. Bertie shot into the hallway, his claws skittering on the polished floorboards. Molly crouched down to stroke him, and let him jump at her and lick her cheek. She couldn't bear to look at Auntie Lucy, in case she was still angry.

"Molly! You shouldn't keep people standing on the doorstep!" Auntie Lucy hurried in, carrying Peter on her hip.

"Hello, Emma." Then Auntie Lucy saw the policeman, who been hidden by the door, and her face drained of colour. The last time someone in uniform had come to the door like this must have been to tell her that her husband had died, Molly realized. She felt even worse, if that was possible. She wasn't sure, but she thought she might be sick.

"It's all right. It's about me. I think," she tried to say, but the words came out half-swallowed, and no one was listening to her anyway.

John and Rose had appeared behind Auntie Lucy now, both looking muddy. Rose was holding a handful of weeds, and she dropped them when she saw the policeman. Not on purpose – they just fell out of her hand. John glanced at Molly, and then away, as if he didn't want to look at her.

"May we come in, Mrs Tolley?" the policeman asked. He wasn't just a constable, Molly noticed, from his uniform. He had more silver on his jacket than Martin's dad did.

"This is Sergeant Duncan," Emma Tennant started to explain. "He's looking for Molly. He thinks he is. I said it couldn't be right. . ."

Auntie Lucy stood back from the door, and they came in, stamping their feet uncomfortably on the mat.

"Go and wash, you two," Auntie Lucy murmured to John and Rose. "Pick up the weeds, Rose. Please." She turned back to Sergeant Duncan and Mrs Tennant. "Can I offer you tea?" she suggested politely.

"Not at the moment, thank you," the policeman rumbled.

Molly stood up, wondering if she should run.

Perhaps that was what Auntie Lucy had meant, telling John and Rose to go back to the scullery and wash. She'd been giving them time to get away. But they were creeping back now, and Auntie Lucy led them all into the front room, where the nicest furniture was. It was a polished sort of room, kept for visitors and special occasions, and full of photographs in silver frames. All of them were staring accusingly at Molly.

"Lucy, I tried to explain to Sergeant Duncan that Molly and John and Rose are your cousin's children," Mrs Tennant said. She was looking anxiously at Auntie Lucy, clearly wanting to be told that she was right, and this was just some strange sort of misunderstanding. One of those odd wartime mistakes.

Auntie Lucy nodded, and then sighed. "No," she admitted. "I'm sorry, Emma, that wasn't actually true. I don't have a Cousin Enid."

"But then where did they come from?" Mrs Tennant demanded, looking bewildered.

Auntie Lucy laughed. "I found them at the bottom of the garden."

"Lucy!"

"I expect she's already told you that I was very badly affected by my husband's death," Auntie Lucy confided to Sergeant Duncan. "Most of the village thinks I'm mad, though of course they'd never say that to my face."

"Not mad, Lucy…" Mrs Tennant said uncomfortably. "But very upset. Of course. And you really mustn't say silly things like that."

"Except I did find them at the bottom of the garden," Auntie Lucy said gently. "John had cut himself on the old cucumber frame. They were in the garden trying to steal apples. It was all they'd been living on for weeks. Apples and blackberries and stolen carrots. They were in a dreadful state."

"We did our best," John muttered. "We couldn't help being dirty."

Sergeant Duncan coughed. "So, to confirm, madam – the children are not your relatives? And

Grant isn't their name? This young lady" – he gestured at Molly, sitting on the sofa with Bertie gripped between her knees – "is actually Molly Mason, of 11 Green Street, London?"

"I don't know." Auntie Lucy shook her head. "They didn't want to tell me their real names. They were hiding."

"And you *let* them?" Molly had never heard Mrs Tennant sound like that. She'd listened to her gossip about village politics for nearly a year, but she never sounded like that. Clearly she was horrified, almost disgusted. "Lucy – how could you be so irresponsible? I've spent all this time telling everyone that you were grieving, and we should be gentle and make allowances, but I just don't understand you! How could you do something so – so *obviously* wrong?"

"It wasn't obvious," Auntie Lucy said tiredly. "They weren't being naughty, Emma. They were exhausted, and starving. It wasn't a silly adventure that I aided and abetted them in. They were running away because they were desperate. Any child who wasn't desperate would have given up after a few days of rain and raw carrots."

"So, you don't know who these two are then?" Sergeant Duncan asked, writing something in his notebook. He eyed John and Rose, looking them up and down. He was working out descriptions for them, Molly realized. *Two children, boy aged around ten, girl aged about six. Dark hair. Brown eyes. Distinguishing marks. . .*

"And the scar on the boy's leg, that's recent then? From falling into the – umm – cucumber frame?" He glanced at Auntie Lucy questioningly.

"I don't know who they are," she agreed. "And yes, the scar is from when he fell."

"We aren't saying," John put in. "You can't make us."

"I'm sure you're on a list somewhere," Sergeant Duncan replied imperturbably, making more notes. "Mrs Tolley, you realize that you've committed an offence? I understand that you misrepresented these children as your relatives, to obtain identity cards for them?"

"Yes," Auntie Lucy replied faintly. "I couldn't give them up. I don't think you would have done either. Not if you'd seen the state of them. You do understand, don't you, that whatever had happened to Rose had left her incapable of speech? She doesn't talk?"

The sergeant looked up, startled out of his official calm. "Not at all?"

"Not ever. I've never heard her speak." Auntie Lucy looked at him. "Would you have made her go back?"

"It isn't for me to say, madam," he told her stiffly. "Mrs Tennant. As the billeting officer for the area – is there anywhere you can temporarily house these two, until we find out where they're meant to be?"

Rose jumped up from the padded stool she and John were sitting on, and flung herself on Auntie Lucy, clinging on so tightly that Peter glared at her, and then began to roar.

"Ssssh, sssh, sssh, there, darling," Auntie Lucy murmured. "It's all right, Rose. It's all right. No one is going to make you go back to those people. I will make absolutely sure of that." She smiled at the sergeant. "My cousin – an actual cousin, this time – is a member of Parliament. I shall telephone him. He has several children of his own, and I can assure you, Sergeant, he will not allow you to return John and Rose to a house where they were cruelly treated."

"The police service does not take kindly to being threatened, Mrs Tolley," Sergeant Duncan said grimly. Then he added, looking at Rose, "Which isn't to say we take kindly to children being badly treated either." He folded up his notebook. "These two. . . They'll have been reported missing, but just now, I'm not looking for a boy and a girl. Only this one." He nodded to Molly. "Your mother's been frantic, you know, miss. Haunting her local station, she is. There every day asking for news."

Molly hung her head. "She was going to kill my dog."

"What?" The sergeant looked at her blankly.

"Bertie. She was going to have him put to sleep."

The sergeant peered down at Bertie, who was now dozing on Molly's feet. He opened one eye as if he realized they were talking about him, and then sat up and wagged his tail slowly.

"He seems a nice enough little thing," the policeman said, reaching out to scratch Bertie's chin. "Some sort of terrier. Good ratter, I expect."

"He is," Molly told him eagerly. "Very good. But he wouldn't eat them. I had to buy him biscuits."

"So you ran away because of the dog?" Sergeant Duncan consulted his notes. "Nothing here about putting him to sleep."

"She was going to, the very next day, she said. She was going to make my sister take him, and our cat too. Or I wouldn't have gone! I couldn't let her do it. Bertie wasn't going to go berserk like they said, he's a *good* dog. I promise. I tried to bring Tom too. He's the cat. But he wouldn't let me."

"The dog's not ill then?" Sergeant Duncan was frowning. "He looks all right."

"There's nothing wrong with him. But there was

a leaflet that said you ought to send your dog to the country, and cats, in case they ran mad because of the bombs. Mum didn't have anywhere to send him, lots of people didn't. You should have seen the line outside Mr France's, he's the vet. It was hundreds of people, honestly."

The sergeant stopped looking at his notes, and eyed Molly, frowning. "Wanting their dogs put to sleep?"

"Cats too. There was a boy with a beautiful black cat. . ." Molly swallowed back tears, thinking of that frightened black cat, and the angry boy, and Perkins. "None of them had anything wrong. They were lovely, just like Bertie."

"Well. I don't know what to say about that, miss." The sergeant tapped his pencil on his notebook. "I don't know what to say at all." Then he straightened his shoulders, and smoothed the front of his uniform tunic. "Still. Your mother's waiting for you at home. Mrs Tennant's said she can accompany you. There's a train. . ."

"You should go and pack your things, Molly," Mrs Tennant told her gently. "We don't have much time."

"Emma, is this really the right thing to do?" Auntie Lucy murmured, and Mrs Tennant looked at her, shocked.

"Of course it is! The child should be with her mother!"

"But so quickly? Can't you give her – us – a little time to say goodbye properly?"

Molly glanced over at her gratefully. She had assumed that Auntie Lucy would be glad to be rid of her, after finding out about her lies. "I have to go," she murmured. "I'll pack now." Her battered little case was in the bottom of the wardrobe in their room.

Rose peeled herself away from Auntie Lucy, and followed her, and Bertie trailed after them, looking confused.

"What about Bertie?" John asked, just as Molly was at the door.

"What about him?" Molly asked tiredly. "Maybe Mum won't do it. She wasn't trying to be cruel, before. It was what everybody said she ought to do. She just did what that booklet said."

"Leave him here." John went to stand by Auntie Lucy's chair. "I'll take him out before we go to school, and for a quick run in the dinner hour. You won't have to do anything. I promise."

"Leave him?" Molly's voice shook.

Of course it was the right thing to do. Bertie would be safe in Marsh End, and happy. John and Rose loved him, and he slept on Auntie Lucy's feet while they were at school. But she had run away to keep her dog. That was what it had all been for. Now she had to give him up?

"I'll look after him." John crouched down to rub Bertie under the chin, and the little dog rolled over and gazed up at him adoringly.

"Even after yesterday?" Molly whispered, her voice choked. "You were so angry with me."

"I'm not going to take that out on Bertie!" John

sounded shocked. He stayed crouched by the dog, fussing with his paws now, and Molly saw that he didn't want to meet her eyes. "Besides, you were only doing it for Rose. I ought to have looked after her better. It's not like I wanted this to happen." He glanced up. "You do know that?"

Molly sniffed. "Sort of."

"Auntie Lucy, we can keep him here, can't we?" John pleaded. "You can't send him back to London to be put to sleep."

"Of course not. We'll look after him, Molly. We'll write to you and tell you how he is." Auntie Lucy got up. "I shall go and help Molly pack," she said to Mrs Tennant and the sergeant. "If you insist on taking her away at once, she'll need time to say goodbye to John and Rose, and Bertie."

"Lucy, it isn't as if we have a choice about it," Mrs Tennant started to protest, but Auntie Lucy was already leading the children upstairs.

*

Mrs Tennant had brought her car to drive them to the station, which just proved how important finding Molly was, with petrol in such short supply. Molly sat in the back, waving to John and Rose and Auntie Lucy. John had Bertie in his arms, and he was making him wave a paw. Molly was almost glad when the little car juddered away – she could hardly see for tears.

They dropped Sergeant Duncan off at the police station in Casley, and then left the car at the railway station – not the one that Molly had arrived at the year before. She still wasn't sure exactly where she had been. Mrs Tennant was fussing, worrying about the tickets, and whether Molly had everything, and how they were to get from Liverpool Street to Molly's house. Molly tried to tell her it wasn't much of a walk, but she was in too much of a panic to listen. She swept Molly through the ticket office, flinging coins around and dropping tickets, and then out on to the platform. They could see the train approaching already, and Mrs Tennant began to fret about how close they'd come to missing it. Molly squeezed herself into an empty corner seat, and turned away from her. It would be more than an hour's journey, and she wasn't sure she could bear to listen to Mrs Tennant's anxious twittering for that long. Luckily the compartment was almost full, and Mrs Tennant was squashed in next to an elderly woman, who eyed Molly and her case with disapproval. Molly felt like telling her that she hadn't wanted to go back to London. It wasn't her idea at all.

It had all happened so quickly that she hadn't had time to think about Mum until now. That she was going to see her in an hour or so, for the first time in more than a year. Molly didn't know what she was going to say. She ought to apologize, she supposed. She pictured her mum at the police station every day, like Sergeant Duncan had said. Desperate for news. For the first time in ages, Molly began to feel guilty. She had been so angry about what Mum was going to do to Bertie, before, but what she had said to John was true, Mum had only been doing the same as everyone else. It didn't make it any better, but it did explain things, a little.

The elderly woman was trying to quiz Mrs Tennant about her now, making barbed little comments about evacuees, and irresponsible mothers who brought their children home. Molly rubbed at her breath on the window, and tried to ignore Mrs Tennant doing her best to be polite and say nothing at the same time. She didn't have a lot of sympathy.

Molly had only been gazing out of the window so as not to get dragged into the conversation, but as they came closer to London, she began to notice the bomb damage. Every so often there was a row of houses with a gap, like a missing tooth. She hadn't imagined whole houses gone, even after that photograph in the paper.

Liverpool Street seemed to be full of people in uniform. Soldiers everywhere, and people with armbands, and tin hats, and a tea stall run by women in WVS green and red. The station was plastered with posters – Molly saw at least three telling mothers not to take their evacuee children home.

"You know the way from here?" Mrs Tennant asked, looking worried again. "Are you sure, Molly? Perhaps we should just take a taxi."

Molly shrugged. "If you're made of money," she muttered. It was rude, but she was past caring now. She was torn between wanting to get home and see the shop and make sure that Mum was safe, and being desperate to go back to Marsh End and Bertie and the others.

Mrs Tennant didn't say anything. She took Molly's case, and smiled at her brightly. "Off you go then. I'll follow along."

Molly started to feel better as they hurried towards the shop. There was hardly any bomb damage to be seen at all. One crater in the middle of the road, with fencing up around, so the cars had to edge by at snail's pace, but there were no missing-tooth houses. Everything did look odd as they came back towards Hanley Road, the shop windows all boarded up to meet the blackout restrictions, and lots of them sandbagged too. Mrs Tennant kept murmuring things like "Goodness!" and "How very strange!" and then "Oh my!" as she saw a silvery barrage balloon floating up above them. But Molly was glad. Everyone was being so careful. They were doing it right, following all the rules. She was breathing a little easier by the time they were a couple of roads away from home.

"Such an odd smell. . ." Mrs Tennant murmured, and Molly glanced back at her, frowning. "The market?" There was a smell of spoiled vegetables, sometimes.

"No. . ." Mrs Tennant caught Molly's arm. "Molly, love, are we close?"

Molly nodded, and then tried to pull away. "Let go. Let go of me!"

"I think we should—" Mrs Tennant started to say, but Molly dragged her arm away and raced off. She could smell it now too. How could she not have noticed? There was smoke in the air, not just from chimneys, but a deeper, darker smell. The air was scratching in her throat, thick with brick dust, and Molly started to cough as she ran.

She turned the corner into Green Street, and stopped. It wasn't there. The end of the street where the shop was, their shop and the ironmonger and the butcher's, just wasn't there. Right in front of her was a huge puddle of dirty water, and where the shops had been was just a pile of blackened bricks and splintered beams. There was a group of firemen standing there with a hose, watching the smoking rubble.

At the other end of the street, across the piles of rubbish, she could see houses that looked just as they always had. Someone was walking down the road with a string bag of shopping, as though it was any other day.

"Molly!" Mrs Tennant dashed round the corner, holding on to her hat, and gasping. "Oh! Oh, Molly. This – this is it?"

Molly shook her head. "It isn't here," she whispered. "My mum's shop. It's supposed to be here."

A man in ARP uniform came picking his way over the rubble. "Stay back, please. Some parts are still smouldering."

"My mum. . ." Molly grabbed his sleeve. "That's our shop."

He frowned down at her worriedly. "You're not Mrs Mason's little girl? The one she was looking for?"

"Yes!" Molly nodded eagerly. "Where is she?" Where did people go when their homes were bombed? She wasn't sure. "Is she still in the shelter?"

"She didn't go to the shelter, lovey," the man said gently. He looked at Mrs Tennant for help, but she was gaping at him in shock. He sighed. "I'm ever so sorry, sweetheart. She was in the house last night when the bomb fell. She's gone."

"No. She was looking for me," Molly told him, shaking her head. If she said it enough, it would be true. "She wanted me back. She was at the police station, that's what the sergeant said. She wanted me to come home, and I did."

Mrs Tennant put an arm around her shoulders. "Molly, let's go. We don't want to be here, not now."

"I do. I'm supposed to be here. She was waiting for me to come back."

"I know, darling. But . . . she isn't here now."

Molly looked round at her. "She isn't *anywhere*."

Mrs Tennant flinched. "She's at peace, Molly. She's not in any pain."

The firemen watching the rubble moved suddenly, two of them crouching down to lift up a heavy beam, and then one of them laughed. Molly watched as another man leaned in, and lifted out something greyish and wriggling. Something that mewed loudly, and then hissed, and tried to scratch the man who'd rescued him.

The grey was only soot and smoke, Molly

realized. Underneath there would be ginger fur. She started to laugh too, ignoring Mrs Tennant's shocked exclamation. She pulled away and started to climb over the shifting bricks, calling, "That's my cat! Please can I have him? It's Tom, it's my cat."

"Off there," the ARP man snapped, picking her up round the waist and snatching her back. "They'll bring the cat. Over here, lads!" he yelled. "Cat belongs to this young lady."

The fireman carried Tom over at arm's length, and looked at Molly doubtfully. "You want him, love? He's a bit of a mess. And he's not happy."

"Yes! Oh, yes." Molly wasn't even sure if Tom would recognize her. She hardly recognized him. He had been such a grand, glossy creature, and now his fur was blackened, and his ears looked ragged. His paws were burnt, she realized as the fireman held him out. He must have been crawling around in the smouldering rubble of the shop, trying to get out, and he'd burned his beautiful creamy-oat-coloured paws.

Molly reached for him gingerly, waiting for him to yowl and dash away, the way he had the last time she'd seen him, but he seemed to know her. She held him the way her mum used to, up against her front with his paws on her shoulder, so he could see all around. He used to sit that way with Mum in the shop sometimes, gazing disdainfully down at Bertie. Tom shifted a little, and one of his singed ears brushed Molly's neck as he laid his chin on his paws.

Molly turned to look at Mrs Tennant. "This is my mum's cat. Wherever you take me, he's coming too. If you don't let me take him, I'll run away and find him. You know I will. I'm not leaving Tom behind again."

Chapter Fifteen

But where were they to take her? No one seemed to know. Molly and Mrs Tennant ended up at the police station, the one where her mum had been every day, asking for news. Molly sat in the little waiting area, imagining her mum standing at that counter, arguing with the weary-looking man shuffling papers behind it. Yesterday they must have told her that they'd found Molly, and she would be home the next morning. Then her mum had gone back to the shop happy, and the bomb had fallen.

There was a mournful yowl from the basket at her feet, and Molly murmured apologetically to Tom. "It won't be long." She didn't know whether it would be long or not, no one had told her what was happening, but she had to say something. Tom was irritating the sergeant behind the counter, and she wasn't going to put her hand in the basket to try and pet him. The scratches on her hand were still oozing blood from the last time she'd tried. And he'd nearly got out. She couldn't risk him disappearing again.

Mrs Tennant came back in to the waiting area, and Molly could see her square her shoulders. More bad news then. She swallowed. "Was Stella there too?" she asked huskily. "Is Stella dead?"

"No! No, Molly, honestly, as far as we know, your sister's fine. It's just that she's nowhere near here." Mrs Tennant sat down next to Molly and closed her eyes for a moment. "She's been assigned to an anti-aircraft battery on the east coast, somewhere. No one wants to tell me exactly where."

"Careless talk costs lives," Molly murmured.

"Well, yes. Except I can't see why it would matter ... still. Someone is going to break the news about your mother to her, and then I expect she'll be given compassionate leave to come and see you."

Molly was silent for a moment. "Come and see me where?" she said eventually.

"I honestly don't know." Mrs Tennant rubbed her eyes. "Your sister is your legal guardian now, but she can't take care of you, not unless she's demobbed, and that's not going to happen. She's too valuable where she is. To be quite honest, Molly, I don't know what to do." She sat up and shook her head. "So, we're going home."

"Home? You mean, back to Marsh End?" Molly jumped up and threw her arms round Mrs Tennant. But then she stepped back, frowning. "Did you ask Auntie Lucy?"

"I haven't, but I'm sure she'll be delighted to have you back." Mrs Tennant picked up Molly's case. "Though I'm not sure how she'll feel about that cat. Come on. I haven't a clue when the next train is, but we may as well get back to the station. At least there might be the chance of a cup of tea," she added, glaring pointedly at the sergeant behind the desk, but he pretended not to hear her.

Molly checked the catches on Tom's basket and picked it up carefully. She was worried about his burnt paws, and she didn't want to shake him about. What *was* Auntie Lucy going to say about an injured, grumpy cat?

She might mind less about Tom than about me, Molly thought miserably as she followed Mrs Tennant out into the street. She still hadn't had a chance to say sorry properly for lying about Rose. Maybe Auntie Lucy wouldn't want her back, after the way she'd dashed her hopes. Molly shivered as she caught the smell of smoke again. *If Rose really could talk to spirits, she could talk to Mum.* She nearly dropped the basket, clutching at it in a panic, and gasping.

"Are you all right, Molly?" Mrs Tennant turned back to look at her. "What is it, dear?"

"Nothing." Molly shook her head. She'd sound strange if she said that she'd only just realized what had happened. That her mother was actually dead. But that was what it felt like. Until now she had been more worried that she'd turned up too late. Like Mrs Tennant fretting about missing a train.

It wasn't that she hadn't understood, more that she hadn't seen what the words meant.

It was dark by the time they got on a train back home, and the blackout blinds were down. The compartment was only lit by a blue-painted bulb, and everyone looked pale and sickly in the dim light. Molly kept trying to peer between the wicker strands of Tom's basket – he wasn't mewing now, and hardly even moving, and she was anxious about him. Worrying about Tom kept her from thinking about Auntie Lucy, but as Mrs Tennant struggled to start the cold car back at Casley Station, Molly couldn't stop herself. What would happen if Auntie Lucy said no? She and Tom would have nowhere to go.

I meant it, Molly thought. *If they send me to a home and I can't take Tom I'll run away and find him*. But she knew deep down that most people would look at a miserable, scruffy cat with burnt paws and think it would be kinder to put him to sleep. By the time she'd run away, there wouldn't be any Tom to rescue.

Even if Auntie Lucy wouldn't take her back, perhaps she'd look after Tom?

The car drew up in the lane, and Molly looked at the house, dark and unwelcoming behind the wall, all its windows blacked out.

"I hope they haven't gone to bed," Mrs Tennant murmured. "Here, pass me the basket."

Molly struggled out of the car, stiff after

sitting cramped in the train. She was so cold, her fingers kept slipping as she tried to take Tom back.

"Emma! I heard the car. Did Molly get home safely? Here, come inside, before Mr Barrett pops up and starts shouting at us about showing a light." Then Auntie Lucy yelped as Bertie shot past her to dance around Molly, leaping up at her and frantically licking her face.

"Molly! Emma, what happened? Couldn't you find her mother?"

"Let's get in out of the cold. Here, just take this while I get Molly's case." Mrs Tennant pushed the basket into Auntie Lucy's arms, and then shepherded Molly in. "Oh, don't put that down on the floor, Lucy, you don't want Bertie getting at it. It's a cat."

Auntie Lucy put Tom's basket on the hall table and shut the door. "Emma, what's going on?" Then she looked at Molly properly. "Sweetheart, what is it? What's happened?"

322

"The shop got hit," Molly whispered. "It's gone. My mum's gone."

"Her sister's in an anti-aircraft battery somewhere, but we don't know where," Mrs Tennant said wearily. "Lucy, can you take her in for now?" She put her hand on Auntie Lucy's arm. "I shouldn't have said those things . . . I don't . . . the house was just bricks, Lucy! Half the street wasn't there. . . I'm sorry. . ."

"She's back!" John was hanging over the banisters. "Rose, Molly's back! Ow, don't push!" he added as Rose barged past him and raced down the stairs.

"I might not be," Molly tried to tell Rose, looking at Auntie Lucy. "I don't know . . . I'm sorry I lied." She was stumbling over her words; she was so cold all over, she could hardly even talk.

"What's the matter with her?" John asked, grabbing at Molly. "Rose, stop hugging her like that, she's not well, she's going to fall over."

Time had to be stopping and starting, Molly decided vaguely. It was as if she'd blinked, and now they were in the kitchen, and she was drinking hot milk with a shawl around her shoulders, and Mrs Tennant and Auntie Lucy talking anxiously over her head.

"But of course, she can stay! I mean, who knows what's going to happen to the three of them, Emma? John's given me his father's address so that I can write and tell him they're here. I think Molly being taken away shocked him into it. I don't see why the father shouldn't let them stay, don't you? I mean, he wanted them safe in the country, and here they are. . ."

"Where's Tom?" Molly murmured, and Auntie Lucy smiled at her.

"I was just about to take that mug off you, I thought you'd fallen asleep! He's here, Molly, look." She turned Molly gently by the shoulders, pointing her so she could see Rose, sitting on the floor behind them with a dish of what looked like chopped boiled egg. There was a nest of blankets next to her, and a greyish-ginger face peering out.

"Come on," Rose said coaxingly. "It's nice, isn't it? Have another bit. You mustn't waste it, I won't get another egg for a week at least."

Her voice was whispery, as though it had faded through not being used, but she was talking, and quite clearly. Molly watched Tom reach over and delicately mouth the piece of egg from between her fingers. Rose's little felt cat was tucked into the blanket next to him.

"What happened?" Molly asked, watching disbelievingly as Rose chattered away to the cat. She'd thought that Rose had given up talking altogether.

John leaned over from the other side of the table. "We opened up the basket and he was so scared, he hissed at me, and sort of flinched back. And then Rose just pushed me out of the way and sat down and started talking to him. She told me to go and get a blanket – it was the first time she'd spoken to me in a year. She and Gran used to feed the old ginger cat from next door, sometimes. I think Tom reminds her of Gran."

Molly jumped as a cold nose pressed against her hand. Bertie was looking up at her hopefully from under the table, and Molly reached down to stroke his nose and fuss over him. "No one's feeding you an egg, are they, I know. It's not fair. . ."

"He knew you'd gone," Auntie Lucy told her. "He sat by the gate all day."

"I had to pick him up and carry him in when we did the blackout," John said.

Molly hoisted Bertie up on to her lap, and let him wriggle inside the shawl. He was a solid little lump of warm, and she buried her cold fingers in his fur. "Do you think he knew I was coming back?"

John shrugged. "He was waiting for *something*."

Auntie Lucy went to see Mrs Tennant out, and

Molly leaned back in her chair. It was just them. The ones who belonged. For now.

"You told Auntie Lucy your address," she remembered suddenly. "She was telling Mrs Tennant. Is that right? You told her how to find your dad?"

John shrugged. "I reckon they found you because of those identity cards. Someone got suspicious. So they're going to come for me and Rose sooner or later. Better to write and tell him, I thought. Then he might let us stay."

"I'll write to Stella tomorrow," Molly said. "That's my sister. She's working on anti-aircraft guns," she added, smiling to herself. Just imagine – her shy, quiet sister, one of those girls in overalls, clambering over a gun. "Like that toy one you got. She might come and visit."

"I'm sorry about your mum," John said awkwardly.

Molly wrapped her arms tighter around Bertie. "I suppose I shouldn't have gone and left her," she said in a small voice. "If I'd been there, she might have gone to the shelter. I'd have made her go. If I was back home just one day earlier, she would have been all right."

"From what you've said about your mum, I reckon you'd both have been in the house." John shook his head. "It would have got you too." He glanced over at Rose. "I don't know what Rose would have done, if that had happened. It wasn't just Bertie waiting for you by the gate, she was out there with him. They were watching for you, even though I tried to explain to Rose that you'd gone back to London. She wouldn't listen."

"Look," Molly whispered. The nest of blankets was shifting slowly as Tom staggered up, limping on his burnt paws. He bumped Rose's chin, and then walked unsteadily across the kitchen floor to Molly. He and Bertie eyed each other suspiciously for a moment, and then Tom went up on his hindquarters, resting his front paws gingerly on Molly's lap.

"He wants you to pick him up," Rose said, coming to watch. She lifted up his back end, and Tom wriggled uncomfortably, slithering on to Molly's lap, and then curling up next to Bertie.

"They never do that," Molly said, her eyes wide. "Never. Tom can't stand Bertie."

Auntie Lucy picked up the blanket and laughed. "That cat knows which side his bread's buttered, Molly."

"He knows he's staying," Rose murmured happily. "We all are, now."

Molly nodded. It wasn't certain – nothing was certain. But they could hope.

Also available from Holly Webb

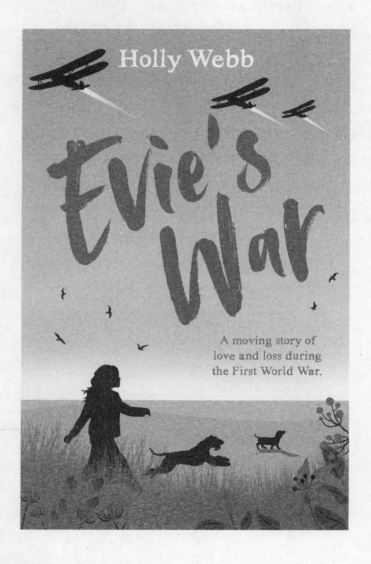

Holly Webb

Evie's War

A moving story of
love and loss during
the First World War.